Film star Carola Russo had the face of a waif, the figure of a wanton, and a million-dollar future. She could do no wrong. Or could she?

Her director didn't want her looking at the wrong men. Her producer didn't want her signing with the wrong studio. Her co-star's jealous wife didn't want her playing the wrong love scenes. Her sexy blond press agent didn't want her making the wrong headlines.

It doesn't take Hollywood operator Rick Holman long to realize that one wrong move could be fatal. And he has to think fast to sort out the sordid motives that lead to a series of movieland murders.

SIGNET Thrillers
by *Carter Brown*

Angel (#S2094—35¢)

The Blonde (#S1972—35¢)

Blonde on the Rocks
(#G2328—40¢)

The Bombshell (#1767—25¢)

The Brazen (#S1836—35¢)

The Corpse (#1606—25¢)

The Dame (#1738—25¢)

The Desired (#1764—25¢)

The Dream Is Deadly
(#S1845—35¢)

The Dumdum Murder
(#S2196—35¢)

The Ever-Loving Blues
(#S1919—35¢)

The Exotic (#S2009—35¢)

Girl in a Shroud
(#G2344—40¢)

The Girl Who Was Possessed
(#G2291—40¢)

Graves, I Dig! (#S1801—35¢)

The Guilt-Edged Cage
(#S2220—35¢)

The Hellcat (#S2122—35¢)

The Hong Kong Caper
(#S2180—35¢)

The Ice-Cold Nude
(#S2110—35¢)

The Lady Is Available
(#S2244—35¢)

The Lady Is Transparent
(#S2148—35¢)

Lament for a Lousy Lover
(#S1856—35¢)

The Lover (#1620—25¢)

Lover, Don't Come Back
(#S2183—35¢)

The Loving and the Dead
(#1654—25¢)

The Million Dollar Babe
(#S1909—35¢)

The Mistress (#1594—25¢)

Murder in the Key Club
(#S2140—35¢)

Murder Wears a Mantilla
(#S2048—35¢)

A Murderer Among Us
(#2228—35¢)

The Myopic Mermaid
(#1924—35¢)

Nymph to the Slaughter
(#G2312—40¢)

The Passionate Pagan
(#S2259—35¢)

The Sad-Eyed Seductress
(#S2023—35¢)

The Savage Salome
(#S1896—35¢)

The Stripper (#S1981—35¢)

The Temptress (#S1817—35¢)

Terror Comes Creeping
(#1750—25¢)

The Tigress (#S1989—35¢)

Tomorrow Is Murder
(#S1806—35¢)

The Unorthodox Corpse
(#S1950—35¢)

The Victim (#1633—25¢)

Walk Softly, Witch
(#1663—25¢)

The Wanton (#1713—25¢)

The Wayward Wahine
(#1784—25¢)

The White Bikini
(#S2275—35¢)

Zelda (#S2033—35¢)

TO OUR READERS: If your dealer does not have the SIGNET and MENTOR books you want, you may order them by mail, enclosing the list price plus 5¢ a copy to cover mailing. If you would like our free catalog, please request it by postcard. The New American Library of World Literature, Inc., P.O. Box 2310, Grand Central Station, New York, New York, 10017.

the *carter brown*
mystery series

the
jade-eyed
jungle

A SIGNET BOOK

published by
THE NEW AMERICAN LIBRARY
OF WORLD LITERATURE, INC.

in association with
HORWITZ PUBLICATIONS INC.

Published by arrangement with Alan G. Yates

FIRST PRINTING, SEPTEMBER, 1963

SIGNET TRADEMARK REG. U.S. PAT. OFF. AND FOREIGN COUNTRIES
REGISTERED TRADEMARK—MARCA REGISTRADA
HECHO EN CHICAGO, U.S.A.

SIGNET BOOKS are published by
The New American Library of World Literature, Inc.
501 Madison Avenue, New York 22, New York

PRINTED IN THE UNITED STATES OF AMERICA

the
jade-eyed
jungle

chapter one

It was a six-story office building, mostly plate glass, and it glittered with reflected sunlight like some enchanted palace that had been transplanted from Hans Andersen onto Wilshire Boulevard overnight. Everything was so *new;* even the brass plate that spelled out CADENZA FILMS, INC. in modern gothic had a kind of virginal aura of unsullied purity. All of it was so light and airy that I was almost afraid to stand anywhere but dead center in the elevator, in case the balance would be upset and it would end up as an architectural curiosity rivaling the original in Pisa.

Finally I found the right office on the fourth floor, and kept clear of the shining lilac walls because the paint didn't even look dry yet. I wondered—obviously this Cadenza outfit had spared no expense in achieving a painless birth—how come they needed a trouble-shooter already, before they were out of the suckling period?

Their director of public relations was sitting in back

of a Scandinavian-designed free-form desk, watching me intently with luminous cobalt-blue eyes. Her short blond hair was carefully brushed back above her ears so it couldn't distract attention from her beautifully moulded face with its high cheekbones, classic nose, and wide curved mouth. The short coat of her champagne-colored silk suit fit tight over her full breasts, and was nipped tighter still to emphasize the contrasting smallness of her waist.

"Mr. Holman?" Her voice was crisp but pleasant. "Won't you sit down? I am Lenore Palmer."

"Thank you." I sat in a Scandinavian-designed arm-chair shaped like an eggshell, and lit a cigarette.

"It's Rick Holman, isn't it?" she asked easily. "Do you mind if we get on a first-names basis right away, Rick?"

"I think that's real friendly, Lenore," I told her.

A hint of steel showed in those big blue eyes for a moment. "You needn't be quite so goddamned sincere about it, Rick," she suggested coldly. "That is, not unless you don't need the money?"

"I always need the money," I said, and this time I was genuinely sincere.

"Good!" The blonde smiled, showing immaculate white teeth. "I should tell you, Rick, it's your reputation in showbiz for handling internal troubles with efficiency and discretion that made me send for you this morning!"

Showbiz! I mentally winced at the word; maybe the blonde had started in the motion picture industry around the same time the building was completed— which looked like yesterday, or maybe the day before, at most.

"It's real nice you've heard of me, Lenore," I said patiently. "You won't think me rude if I mention I've never heard of you, or Cadenza Films, either?"

She smiled again, or maybe she just bared those white teeth at me. "You've heard of Aria Productions,

Rick? And I'm sure you've heard of Aria's former president, Mr. Oscar Neilsen?"

"Sure," I agreed. "Who hasn't?"

"Cadenza Films is an offshoot from Aria, under the personal supervision of Mr. Neilsen," she said in a faintly condescending tone. "Maybe you've never heard of me, because I've been in Europe the last four years as Mr. Neilsen's press secretary."

"His press secretary?" I kept my voice strictly neutral. "That must have been loads of fun!"

"Don't get flip with me, buddy boy!" she said with icy contempt. "Oscar Neilsen never makes the mistake of trying to mix pleasure with business, especially with the front office help! I hope I make myself very clear?"

"You do," I admitted. "I also think Mr. Neilsen shows himself to be a fathead, too."

"Don't butter me up either," she said impatiently. "We'll get along together just fine if you remember we both have a job of work to do—and do it!"

"It was a genuine compliment," I explained carefully. "You must know you're a very attractive woman, Lenore—or else your myopic pride won't let you wear glasses?"

She took a deep breath. "All right, let's forget it! We're just wasting time this way. I would be grateful, Rick, if you'd confine your remarks to the business at hand in future. I guess you should know now—before you start working for me—that I'm one of those eager-beaver executive types who just hates to waste even one whole minute during the day's work. So make yourself a listener while you're in my office and we'll get along like a couple of lovebirds in full-throated golden song!"

"Just so long as I let you do all the singing, or else all your pretty feathers will get ruffled?" I said.

"It sounds tough, I know."

I wondered at the sudden gruff note in her voice, then realized she was striving for that buddy-buddy approach of the bossman in a sanitation crew, when he wants his boys to get with it while they're working the main sewer.

"Don't worry, Rick." The white teeth flashed at me again. "You'll find I'm not such a bad old bitch to work for after a while!"

"I just had a hot flash," I said in an awed voice. "The mortgage payment is already met this month—I don't really need the money after all."

"What is that supposed to mean, exactly?" The luminous eyes held a faintly puzzled look.

"It means I'm not about to be emasculated, not even by a lovebird in full-throated golden song," I told her carefully. "I wouldn't mind working for a genuine bad old bitch, but you're a gold-plated young bitch and they're the worst kind." I got up from the chair and smiled down at her white face. "Go play your cadenza in somebody else's ear, honey, because suddenly I'm tone-deaf!"

I had almost reached the door when she said *"Wait!"* in a muffled voice. Politeness being a Holman characteristic, I turned back and caught the full impact of the murderous fury in her cobalt-blue eyes. Her face was chalk-white, and two bright red spots burned high on her cheeks.

"Sit down, you—you thin-skinned bastard!" She almost choked getting the words out. "Hasn't your Cro-Magnon bird-brain realized you're living in the twentieth century yet? Don't you understand that women have equal rights now? They demand something more from life than spending their days over a hot stove and getting an occasional reward of a roll in the hay from their lord and master. Who the hell do you think you are to walk out on me before I—?"

"Why didn't you tell me it was that kind of deal?" I interrupted her eagerly. "Lenore, honey! I'll be happy to look after your hot stove for that kind of occasional reward! Tell you what! I'll lock the door—you take your clothes off—and we're in business!"

For a moment there I figured she'd simply disintegrated; then she suddenly slumped back in her chair and made a thin howling noise. It took me a while to realize she was laughing.

"Okay!" she said in a weak voice some time later. "I apologize, Rick, so sit down again. I spent the last two years in Rome, and if you don't talk that way the whole time the Italians keep right on pinching your behind, even if you're facing them at the time!"

I sat down again but it was against my better judgment. Lenore Palmer dabbed her eyes with a minute handkerchief and quickly regained her former composure, only this time it wasn't so obviously obnoxious.

"How come you have a problem, what with Cadenza Films being such a brand-new outfit and all?" I queried.

"It's inherited," she said. "Mr. Neilsen had a wonderfully brilliant idea. He's always been a loyal, one hundred per cent American, so for him runaway production in Europe is out—"

"Especially right now when it costs as much as it does at home?" I added helpfully.

She let that one wither all by itself.

"But, Mr. Neilsen appreciated that a lot of the European stars have become very big in their own right," Lenore continued enthusiastically. "So he had this positively scintillating new idea. He'd import the talent and have them make motion pictures right here in Hollywood. Then he created his own organization to handle the deal—that's Cadenza."

"And that's Carola Russo?" I said. "I remember reading about her in the trade papers. She arrived about a month back?"

"She did." The wide mouth turned down at the corners expressively. "She's the problem, Rick. Her producer came with her—Gino Amaldi."

"Isn't he also her husband?"

"In every sense but the dictionary definition of the word," Lenore said, shrugging. "He already had a legal wife before he ever met Carola, and short of a divorce

Italian-style, he'll never be able to legalize the union with Carola."

"Don't they have one of those Trilby-Svengali relationships that seem to be so big in Europe these days?" I queried. "He was the big producer who discovered her and built her into a star, so now she dotes on him to the point where she wouldn't even think of taking a glass of orange juice without his prior permission—that kind of jazz?"

"You are exactly right," she said crisply, "up until about three weeks back! Then she met Don Gallant who's playing opposite her in the picture and—*Bingo!*" There was a look of genuine wonderment in those luminous eyes. "It was like nuclear fission, five minutes after they'd met you could almost hear Gallant sizzling, and Carola was loving him to death with those jade-green eyes of hers already! Then, a couple of days later, Amaldi had to go back to Rome for some final editing on his last picture, and that left Carola free, and like uninhibited. Even Mr. Neilsen himself noticed what was going on between her and Gallant!"

"Mr. Neilsen sounds like a real sharp guy," I said in an admiring voice.

"Oscar Neilsen is a genius." The flat tone of Lenore's voice defied contradiction. "But there was still one little problem holding Gallant back—"

"His wife?" I suggested wearily.

"Oh, but I can see you've been here before, Rick!" She grinned sourly. "His wife—Monica Hayes—the girl who always gets those trusting, ever-loving little wife parts in television dramas. In real life she's so trusting, she dusts off all his mail before she gives it to him, then checks the fingerprints with the F.B.I. But Don got a break; Monica had a second lead in a B-western and went on location to Colorado a few days after Amaldi had gone back to Rome. Only then the two of them discovered they had a brand-new problem—Mr. Neilsen. He made sure they never had a chance to be alone together by sacrificing his own leisure; he kept himself at Carola's side the whole time."

"Mr. Neilsen's not only a genius, he's all heart, too?" I said respectfully. "I'm impressed."

"That worked fine up until three days back," Lenore grated. "Then the both of them suddenly disappeared."

"You mean Carola and Mr. Neilsen?" I asked innocently.

"You know goddamn well who I mean!" she snapped. "This is no time to get cute, Rick, we have a serious problem here. The two of them simply disappeared into thin air—and that was only the start of it! Amaldi got back from Rome a week earlier than he'd anticipated, and he's been foaming at the mouth for the last twenty-four hours. Monica Hayes' location unit had perfect weather in Colorado and not one scene took more than three takes, so she also arrived back early and found a nice empty house waiting for her. The way she's sounding off would make a stevedore who's just buried a steel hook in his own foot, sound like T. S. Eliot giving a poetry reading for a few select friends!"

"So any minute now she'll blow sky-high and give some eager Hollywood reporter the whole story?" I said.

"Exactly right!" For a moment that beautifully molded face looked gaunt at the thought.

"I'm confused," I told her. "One of us is out of his mind. I guess it has to be you."

"How's that?"

"You got a big problem you tell me," I muttered. "You—with a stenciled sign on your door that says you're the director of public relations yet! What problem? Once Monica Hayes talks to the papers you've got a million dollars' worth of publicity going for the movie, for free!"

"Don't!" Lenore shuddered visibly, and taut, champagne silk bounced delightfully. "If a word of this ever gets out Mr. Neilsen will slit my throat! It would ruin the whole deal with Amaldi, and the picture is nothing without Carola Russo playing the lead. Mr. Neilsen has two hundred thousand already committed and if he doesn't have the Russo dame, all that money's flushed straight down the john! You've got to find her, and Don Gallant, and get the two of them back here real fast, Rick!"

"They've been gone three days already?" I said bleakly. "But it's only now you've thought about having someone go look for them?"

"Mr. Neilsen was most upset when it happened, naturally," she said. "But he was sure they'd be back before the others. The horror of it all is that the Russo dame doesn't expect Amaldi to be here until next week, and Gallant's convinced his wife is still on location in Colorado. Once they know what's happened you won't have any trouble in getting them to come back real fast, Rick."

"The trick is to find them first," I reminded her. "How do you know they're together?"

"Mr. Neilsen had a script conference that night, so he left Carola on her own for a couple of hours in her hotel suite," Lenore explained. "When the conference was finished he went up to her suite and found she'd gone. The desk clerk told him Mr. Gallant had arrived about an hour back, called her room, and she left with him ten minutes later, carrying an overnight case."

"They wouldn't want to be seen in public together in case they were recognized," I said, using the obvious logic first. "The Russo dame is on her first visit so it would be up to Gallant to find them a nice quiet hide-away."

"Keep going!" She had a fatuous look of expectancy on her face, like Holman would resolve the whole problem in two minutes flat.

"With Amaldi in Europe and his wife on location, Gallant would figure they didn't need to worry about anybody chasing after them?"

"He'd know Mr. Neilsen would never demean himself, or Cadenza Films, by instituting some kind of cheap manhunt," she said with great dignity.

"So all Gallant needed was a hideaway that guaranteed privacy and kept them safe from accidental recognition by John Q. Public?"

"I guess that's right, Rick."

"Maybe he owns a shack on some quiet beach someplace?" I suggested. "Or a li'l ole log cabin up in the mountains—a tent built for two that nestles under some lonesome pine?"

"I don't know, but I sure as hell can find out!" Her eyes gleamed as she grabbed for the phone.

After some crisp conversation to some girl called Dolly—I hoped it was a girl, anyway, because Cadenza Films had enough problems already—then a long wait followed by a little more crisp conversation, Lenore put down the phone. If I had been right out of my mind I could have suspected the look in her eyes was one of admiration.

"The li'l ole log cabin in the mountains," she said breathlessly. "I'll write down the directions on how to get there that Dolly gave me, so you can't go wrong." She wrote busily on a scratch pad, then tore off the sheet and pushed it across the desk toward me. "You should have them back here by this afternoon. You're a genius, Rick! Solved the whole problem right here in front of my very eyes, like that!" She snapped her fingers expertly in triumph.

"It was kind of stupid of me," I said gloomily. "Now you'll scream when you see the size of my bill."

"You have Carola Russo and Gallant back where they belong by this afternoon, and nobody will be about to raise an eyebrow at the size of your bill," she said confidently. "Good fortune go with you, my brave knight!"

I waited until I had the door open, then turned and leered at her suggestively.

"You just keep tending the stove while I'm gone, fair lady," I told her, "and have the hay spread ready for when I return."

Lenore Palmer's luminous eyes leered right back at me with startling ribaldry dancing in them. "I'm still the same gold-plated executive-type bitch, even when it comes to a roll in the hay," she said throatily. "You sure you wouldn't be scared to death already before you had a chance to catch hay fever?"

chapter two

A couple of hours later, I found the log cabin clinging hopefully to a precipitous slope on the low side of a back mountain road. When I stopped the car it made the third in line parked out front of Don Gallant's hideaway. What the hell, I thought wildly, maybe he's the president of the secret lovers' league and they're holding the annual convention at his hideaway this year.

The first car in line was a heart-stopping white Gia sports, which was empty; the second was a Thunderbird convertible with the top down, and a girl sitting in the front passenger's seat, watching me with an expression of mild curiosity on her face. I got out of my own car and walked down the line toward her.

She had the kind of natural dark brown hair I thought had gone out of style because you hardly see it around any more, and it looked good, swept away behind her left ear on one side and making a soft half-frame for her pixie face on the other. Her eyes were an intelligent hazel, her nose delicately tiptilted; her lips

were full and sensual only when she wished them to be,
I guessed. A white cotton-knit blouse swelled with the
confident thrust of high breasts, and a tailored charcoal
rayon skirt smoothly contained generous hips and firm
thighs.

"Let me guess." She closed her eyes for a moment.
"I know! You're a sex maniac taking inventory."

"I'm looking for Don Gallant," I said, "but nobody
told me it was a group project."

She studied my face intently for a couple more
moments, then shook her head gently. "You can't be
his wife—she's in there already engaged in the same
quest, and from the ominous quiet that's been coming
from inside that shack for the last ten minutes, I'd say
she hasn't found him yet."

"I'm Rick Holman," I told her in a bleak voice.
"His studio hired me to find him first, before anything
like this happened."

"Oh, well"—she smiled cheerfully—"maybe you'll
win the next one?"

"Who are you?" I queried.

"A friend of the deserted wife, giving moral support
through the long drive from Bel Air up here." Her
lower lip drooped in an incredible burlesque of a close-
up shot of the woman scorned, which can be seen
almost any night on the small screen. "You don't know
the heartbreak of it all," she murmured piteously.
"They spent their honeymoon right here in that little
shack—the same shack in which Monica now suspects
her erring husband is skulking because he's been
shacked up with a little piece of Italian pizza the last
few days!"

"I guess I'll go on in and pick up whatever's left,"
I grunted.

"Fine!" she said with obvious enthusiasm. "I'll go
with you. I've been waiting for a halfway excuse to
rubberneck and you're it, friend."

When she stood beside me she was taller than I'd
figured. The stiff breeze off the mountain top whipped

her skirt against her legs and they were shapelier than I'd figured.

"Rick Holman?" she asked.

"That's right."

"See what a superb memory I've got?" She smiled complacently at me. "I never forget a name—it's only faces that bother me. I'm Janie Trent. When I'm not busy suffering helpfully with a friend what's been done wrong, I'm in television selling soap."

"Soap?" I said.

"Well, detergents mostly," she admitted. "About every time you see a pair of hands plunge into a dish-washing orgy and emerge just as beautiful as they ever were because of the magic ingredients of the sponsor's product—they're my hands you're watching, friend!"

"It sounds like a ball," I muttered.

"Let me tell you I have the best hands in the business," she said proudly. "I also have a couple more assets I figure aren't half bad either, but that's only a personal opinion. You want to hear more?"

"You're just the kind of distraction I need right now," I said, then grabbed her elbow and gently steered her toward the shack.

"I'm twenty-three years old, unmarried but not without a certain amount of judicious experience," she continued in a conversational voice. "Never wear a girdle because they make me itch, sleep in the raw be-cause you never know but what some tall handsome secret agent might take refuge in my apartment one night, and I like to drink rye when I'm drinking. My figure's even better than you think it is, but I'm the intellectual type really—you should see my list of all the good books I've never read! And—I just know you were about to ask!—no, my glamorous career in television hasn't altered me one little bit. I'm still exactly the same kookie bitch I ever was."

By the time she paused for breath we had reached the rustic porch. The front door was wide open, and all I could hear from inside the shack was the same ominous silence Janie Trent had already mentioned.

"How about you?" She had her breath back in no time at all.

"I'm only an unlucky guy who just joined the ranks of the unemployed," I growled. "Let's go find out what kind of mayhem your friend, the cheated wife, has created in there."

The open door led straight into the living room of the shack which was furnished in an expensive, late 1950's rustic style—around the time the Gallants spent their honeymoon here I guessed. For a moment, the two women looked frozen in a tableau there in the center of the room, then they both turned their heads and glared at us savagely.

Carola Russo was the one sprawled carelessly in an armchair with her red hair tumbling around her shoulders; the jade-green eyes that smoldered with a sullen fury identified her for sure. So the brunette who stood scowling down at her, arms folded tight beneath her outraged bosom, had to be the cheated wife, Monica Hayes.

"What the hell do you want?" the brunette grated. I figured if a casting director could have seen her right then, she would never get to play that trusting ever-loving little wife bit again.

"Monica, honey," Janie Trent said easily. "This is Rick Holman. The studio sent him—so I figured maybe I should come with him in case you needed any moral support."

The look of naked ferocity Monica Hayes gave me right then would have curled the hair of a Samson, never mind a Holman.

"So?" She spat the word at me. "When Neilsen knows I'm back he suddenly gets remorse, huh? It didn't worry him my husband was playing house up here with this piece of foreign garbage, not while I was safely out of the way in Colorado, huh? But when he finds out I'm back earlier than expected, *then* he starts worrying about his actor's morals! Well, you can tell him from me that this is going to make a real big story in tomorrow's papers, coast to coast! I'm going to blast him wide open—bury him even—with the kind of stinking publicity that'll dig a nice deep grave big enough for him, that cheating bum I married, and this two-bit alley cat. The three of them side by side, and will I ever enjoy shoveling the dirt down onto their sniveling faces!"

She transferred her venomous stare from me to the redhead sprawled in the armchair. The Italian girl sneered back at her contemptuously, then said something short and sharp that made the air crackle. Her meaning was explicit, even if I didn't know the language; I could see from the way her face suddenly flamed a bright red, that Monica Hayes felt the same way about it, too.

"Where is Don?" Janie Trent asked brightly, maybe two seconds before the tension between the other two women exploded into physical violence.

"He's not here," Monica snapped. "I've looked all over, but he's vanished someplace. Maybe he saw me coming and leaped out the window." Her eyes gleamed brightly at the thought. "He could be lying there in the valley right now with a busted neck, I hope!"

"Doesn't she know where he is?" Janie gestured toward Carola Russo.

"How would I know?" Monica grated. "I don't talk spaghetti talk, do you?"

Janie shook her head, then looked at me questioningly.

"I don't speak any Italian, either," I admitted.

"Do you want to wait for him, honey?" Janie asked.

"I guess not," Monica said reluctantly. "If he saw me coming, he's halfway back to Beverly Hills by now!" The outraged bosom suddenly heaved. "I was about to give Lucrezia Borgia here something to remember me by when you came in, like a busted lip. But I guess the publicity will do a better job, at that!"

"Mrs. Gallant—Miss Hayes," I said nervously. "Don't

you think you should wait until you've calmed down a little—had a chance to think it over—before you do anything you might regret later?"

Her outraged scorn clouted me like the back of a hand across my face. "You creep!" she whispered harshly. "You not only look like one of Neilsen's broken-down flacks, you even talk like one! You go back to little Caesar and tell him from me he'd better start packing his bags ready to get out of town fast— the avalanche is coming!" She glared down at the red-headed girl again. "And while you're at it, take this with you and drop it down the nearest sewer where it belongs!"

Carola Russo made the air crackle with what sounded like the same thing she'd said before, only this time she punctuated it by pursing her lips and giving a Bronx cheer. The brunette paled for a moment, then started toward her with an air of murderous determination. Janie Trent made a kind of standing jump, grabbed Monica's arm, and hauled her toward the door. When they reached it, Janie pushed the cheated wife out onto the porch first, then turned and gave me a warm, sympathetic smile.

"I don't think you look like one of Neilsen's broken-down flacks, Rick Holman," she said softly. "Even if you do talk like one."

Then they were gone. I listened until the sound of the Thunderbird died away in the distance, and the silence inside the room got louder with every passing second. I walked across to the armchair where Carola Russo was still sprawled in a kind of relaxed insolence, and offered her a cigarette. She took one and I held the match while she lit it.

"Thanks." She blew a cloud of smoke into my face. "I thought that stupid fat cow would never go!"

I gaped at her blankly: "I thought you only spoke one language—Italian?"

"Perhaps the cow was right about you?" She blew another cloud of smoke into my face. "If you were a good flack you'd know I was a little English starlet who hadn't had any luck in London, and was hoping to blossom to stardom in Rome, when Gino Amaldi discovered me! Don't you ever read your own press releases?"

"I'm not any kind of flack," I told her, "not that it matters. Why did you put on that, 'No speak English' bit for Monica Hayes?"

"It was the easiest way out of an embarrassing situation," she said wearily, "a dangerous one, too! You don't look like a bloody fool—to borrow from the cow's phrase—so why talk like one, Mr. Holman?"

She got up out of the armchair in a supple flowing movement that was purely feline, and stretched her arms over her head. "I need a drink!"

It gave me a chance to take a real good look at Carola Russo for the first time since I'd walked inside the shack. She had the face of a waif, orphaned and lost in a cruel hard world. A slim boyish figure was contradicted by the arrogant tilt of her breasts, which looked bigger than they were because of the contrast to her slender hips. Her every movement, however minute, was completely feminine and feline. She exuded sex with the kind of contemptuous disregard for its effect that meant she'd been born that way. Now it had become simply a part of her everyday life, like eating, sleeping, taking a shower.

The black silk shirt, with the gold monogram sitting snugly on the firm slope of her left breast, was crumpled as if she'd slept in it the previous night. Her black Capri pants, which had a metallic silver thread woven through the fabric, were so tight they might have been glued straight onto her bare skin. When she walked away from me toward the bar, I figured Gino Amaldi hadn't been such a genius in discovering her star potential after all. Only a blind man could have missed it.

She made herself an outsized drink and swallowed half of it in one long gulp before she turned back toward me with the glass in her hand.

"I needed that!" The strain showed in haunted eyes, as if she was forever trapped in a jade-green jungle with the implacable hunter ceaselessly stalking her—his predestined prey—just beyond the range of vision.

"What did happen to Don Gallant?" I asked her.

"The cow's friend said you were from the studio?" Her voice was suspicious with a strong undertone of fear, verging on hysteria. I was surprised a second-rate actress like Monica Hayes—even if she was playing her cheated-wife bit for real this time—could have scared a girl like Carola Russo that bad. I explained who I was and how Cadenza Films, through Lenore Palmer, had hired me to bring her and Gallant back to town real fast in the hope it could be done before Monica Hayes and Amaldi discovered where they were.

"Gino?" She sucked her breath in with a hissing sound. "Gino is back?"

"A week earlier than he expected," I quoted Lenore Palmer. "He's been foaming at the mouth the last twenty-four hours."

She closed her eyes for a moment as a shudder seized her whole body, then she gulped down the rest of her drink.

"How about Gallant?" I came back to my original question. "Where in hell did he get to?"

"He's under the house," she whispered.

"I'll go tell him he can come out now, his wife's been gone five minutes already!" I sneered.

"He can't come out." She pressed the back of her hand against her mouth and bit fiercely into the skin, before she added the clincher. "He's dead!"

"Dead?"

"That was why I was so scared the whole time she was here," she continued in the same whispering voice. "I thought she was going to kill me, too!"

"You mean Monica Hayes killed him?" There was a kind of squeaky edge to my own voice, I suddenly realized. "How the hell did it happen?"

"Don has a kind of workroom built under the back of

the house. He did a couple of hours' work down there this morning while I slept late. I went down to tell him it was time we had a drink and he came outside, then—" she bit her lower lip sharply "then there was a shot and Don fell backwards into the workshop with blood all over him! I was going to him, when there was another shot and I heard the bullet hit the doorframe right beside me. I knew whoever it was, was trying to kill me, too, so I just panicked and ran inside the house."

I took the glass out of her trembling hand and moved in beside her to the bar while I made her another drink.

"I didn't know what to do!" She chewed her knuckle again in a kind of despair. "There was the phone right there in the corner but who could I call? Then I heard her footsteps outside and before I could do anything, she walked right into the room. She didn't have the gun where I could see it, so I thought maybe she was going to hit me first. I threw myself into the armchair like a little kid trying to hide where there's no place to hide!"

"What did she say?"

"She kept on calling me all the dirty words she could think of, saying them over and over again," Carola said dully. "After a while she just dried up. Then she asked where was her husband and I knew it was some kind of a trick, so I pretended I only spoke Italian and didn't know what she was talking about. She stamped around the place—into the bedroom and the bathroom—then she opened the back door and looked but she didn't go outside. I thought she would go down to the workshop perhaps, to make sure she had killed Don, but she didn't, she came back to me and just stood there with her eyes hating me all the time. I was sure she was building up her hatred to the point where she'd shoot me, too—then you and her girlfriend came in."

"I'll go take a look at the workshop." I pressed the

new drink into her hand. "Drink that, I won't be gone more than a couple of—"

"What was that?" Her pupils dilated with sudden terror.

I listened for a few seconds, then heard it myself—a faint scuffling sound coming from somewhere outside the back of the cabin. I turned around and had gotten three steps closer to the back door when it suddenly crashed wide open.

"Don!" Carola's voice was a thin scream.

A tall dark-haired guy staggered into the room and stood there swaying on his heels gently, his hand clutched to his left shoulder only partially covering the dark wet stain that soaked his shirt.

"Oh, Don!" Carola gasped. "I thought you were dead!"

"I—" Gallant said thickly. "I—" His knees suddenly buckled under him and he crashed full-length onto the floor.

chapter three

Carola lay back in the armchair, her hands interlocked in her lap, her eyes closed tight. I walked past her on my way from the bar to the couch, where Lenore Palmer sat bolt upright, her back rigid with job insecurity. She took the drink from me without saying anything, her gaunt face immersed in her own problems.

The bedroom door opened and Oscar Neilsen stepped out into the living room, then carefully closed the door shut again behind him. By the time he turned around, Carola was sitting up straight with her eyes wide open. and Lenore was on her feet positively quivering to go to work on behalf of her genius employer.

"The doctor says there is nothing to worry about," Neilsen announced softly, his perfect articulation obviously having a soothing effect on both his feminine listeners. "It's only a flesh wound, the bullet went clean through his shoulder and out the other side. The doctor also offers praise for your efforts, Holman, before he arrived. You did a good job in cleaning the wound and staunching the bleeding, he says."

He moved across to the center of the room and stared hard at Carola for a few seconds without speaking. You could feel the power of his personality dominating the silence. With his neatly brushed white-gray hair and suntanned, unwrinkled face, Oscar Neilsen looked like some kind of modern-day saint. The impression was enhanced by the mild tolerance that showed in his clear blue eyes, and the beautifully modulated deep bass voice. The only thing wrong with the impression was that nobody could have carved themselves the kind of niche in Hollywood he had, and retained even a remote resemblance to any kind of saint, modern-day or otherwise.

"Carola, my dear, I want you to listen carefully!" He smiled warmly at her. "I explained to the doctor that Don was cleaning his gun when it accidentally went off—"

"Cleaning his gun?" She stared at him blankly. "He wasn't cleaning his gun! It was that crazy wife of his! She tried to kill him—and me! She should be put away somewhere and—"

"Calmly, my dear!" He rested his hand on her shoulder as if to reassure her, and she winced with sudden pain. "It is vital to all of us that the truth remains our secret. If it ever got out, it could be ruinous."

"But she'll try again!" Carola whispered fearfully.

"I shall see to it that she doesn't," he said easily. "Compose yourself, my dear. Any moment Amaldi will arrive and then your troubles will be over."

"Gino—coming here?" Her eyes wept unshed tears as she looked inward, back toward the terror of her own jade-green jungle.

"After what happened, I had no choice but to tell Gino the whole story," Neilsen said sympathetically. "He is a very understanding man, my dear, very understanding!"

"Gino?" Her mouth twisted derisively.

Neilsen had already forgotten her as he moved away toward his director of public relations. Lenore twitched painfully as he came close.

"This is entirely your fault, you stupid bitch!" he said pleasantly. "I told you last night to take care of it, get Holman to handle the detail—he has a reputation for these things! But for some peculiar reason of your own, you let it wait until this morning—why?"

"I'm desperately sorry, Mr. Neilsen!" Lenore said in a shaking voice. "It was late when you mentioned it —after five—and somehow I automatically thought about it as a business matter to be handled in business hours."

"You're losing your mind." There was a clinical detachment in his voice. "Old maids' traumas, probably— your sexual fantasies transcending reality and destroying your judgment. You don't get any younger, you know!"

"I'm sorry, Mr. Neilsen," she said in a choked voice, "so desperately sorry!" The stricken look on her face said she was slowly bleeding to death inside. "What can I do?"

"You've done enough already. I'll have to undo it!" he said curtly. "You remember Gallant's home number?"

She gave it to him without hesitation and he nodded briefly before he went across to the phone. His audience of three watched expectantly while he dialed the number, a slightly bored expression on his face as he waited for someone to answer.

"This is Oscar Neilsen,' he said crisply, a couple of seconds later. "It is imperative that I speak with Mrs. Gallant at once." Then he waited again, his body completely relaxed, like a man with nothing more on his mind than a call to his nearest liquor store to have them send up a fresh bottle of Scotch.

"Monica?" He yawned gently while he listened to her for a few seconds. "You have a filthy mouth, so close it and listen to me!" There was a new icy sound in his deep bass voice. "I presume you will deny everything I say, so I shall recount a sequence of events to you, and you will refrain from interjecting the usual inanities of denial and surprise while I speak!"

He retold Carola's story of the shooting and how Monica had appeared right after the panic-stricken girl had gotten back inside the cabin, and then pretended to Monica she spoke nothing but Italian because she was in fear of her life. Then he added the news that her husband was far from dead, in fact had only a slight flesh wound which they had told the doctor happened accidentally while he was loading his gun.

"If one word of your husband's interlude with Carola Russo in the mountains leaks out to the press," Neilsen continued conversationally, "I promise you you'll be charged with attempted murder, and I shall make it my personal task to see you are convicted!"

He listened blandly for a few more seconds, then smiled beatifically "My dear Monica, there are a dozen or more people who'd be delighted to swear on oath they were there at the time and saw you fire the gun at your husband with their own eyes! If it comes to a point, I have a couple of bit-players under contract who would be delighted to testify that they were having a rather sordid triangular affair with you at the time you tried to murder your husband! For the promise of featured parts in my next production I'm sure they'd volunteer to murder you even, if that is my wish."

His smile broadened as he listened to her again. "I'm so glad you're being sensible, my dear. The doctor will bring Don home to you in a private ambulance sometime this evening, and I'll see to it he has professional nursing care from the moment he arrives home. I'll wait until he's back in the arms of his brave little wife before we break the story. Better wash off your makeup before the reporters arrive so you can look brave but cheerful for them. I want to see you come out of this well, my dear!"

He hung up, then looked at Lenore. "You stay here

and travel back in the ambulance with Gallant and the doctor. Once you're sure everything is set up right—get a sexy-looking nurse holding a thermometer or something in the background—break the story to the newspapers."

"Yes, Mr. Neilsen," she said dully.

"And smile! For the kind of money I'm praying you, you can look enthusiastic!"

"Yes, sir!" Her wide mouth curved tremulously into a grotesque parody of a smile. "I'll see this story gets the best goddamn coverage possible!"

"That's better."

Rapid footsteps sounded on the front porch, then a rotund bundle of nervous energy burst into the room.

"It's all right, Gino," Neilsen said easily. "Everything is under control."

"So?" Gino Amaldi came to a sudden stop about six feet inside the door. He was a short fat man with a completely bald head that looked like it was shaven. He waited to regain his breath while his sunken, soiled-looking brown eyes carefully searched Neilsen's face, as they estimated just how much truth was contained in that reassuring statement that everything was under control.

Neilsen shrugged resignedly and gave him chapter and verse—Gallant's gun wound was minor and caused by an accident, Monica Hayes would keep her mouth shut and play ball. Everything was roses.

"So?" The fat little man nodded sagely when Neilsen had finished. "Is good. No fuss, no scandal, we still have our great motion picture before us."

"All before us, my friend," Neilsen said softly. "I think you should take Carola straight back to the hotel. She is very disturbed by all the unpleasantness she has suffered."

Amaldi nodded again, then walked toward the armchair, bouncing up and down as he went like there were springs in his elevator shoes. It should have looked hilarious, like something out of the bygone era of slapstick comedy, but it didn't look even remotely amusing —maybe because of the implied menace in his hunched shoulders and the rigidity of the fat neck that bulged over his collar.

He stopped directly in front of the armchair and looked down at Carola for a long moment, then held out his arms open wide.

"Cara mia!" His voice was a caress.

There was a dragging reluctance in the way she slowly got up from the chair, her face completely devoid of expression. Face to face, she was three inches taller than the Italian producer, in spite of his elevator shoes. There was an uneasy contrast between Amaldi's bulk and the girl's slender body as they stood close together looking into each other's eyes.

"Gino—"

His fleshy lips parted in a slow smile. "Now you make Poppa Gino look the fat little old fool that he is, why are you not laughing, *cara?* It is a good American joke?"

"Gino—" She half-raised her arm in a vague gesture of supplication, then suddenly changed her mind and let it drop back to her side. "Gino—please don't!"

"Four days and four nights," he said thickly. "The man was tall—with so much black hair!—handsome and virile. Even the name—Gallant—was so right for you, *cara.* Who needs funny little Poppa Gino and his ugly bald head any more?" He tugged the bulbous tip of his nose with sudden impatience. "I tell you who needs him, *cara,* it's you! Without Poppa Gino you are a nothing again—back where I found you!" He shook his head in a slow, ponderous movement. "You must never forget it, *cara!* Without me you are a nothing."

He lifted his right arm high, then swung it toward her face in an unhurried, powerful movement. She saw it coming and had plenty of time to duck, but she chose to stand and wait for it in a rigid unmoving stance. The back of Amaldi's hand smashed against her cheek with an explosive report, and the power behind the blow drove her sideways onto her knees.

"You must never forget, *cara*," he repeated softly. "Up to your feet again because there are three more times to come. That will make one for each day you spend with the Gallant, so that you always remember you belong to Poppa Gino!"

Carola lurched back onto her feet and faced him again, one side of her face discolored by an angry crimson blotch. Amaldi raised his right arm again with the same unhurried deliberation.

"Hit her one more time, little man," I said coldly, "and I'll break your arm!"

"It is none of your business," he said in a completely indifferent voice. "It is between the green-eyed Galatea and the one who created her—me!"

His arm swung toward her face again so I lunged forward. I gripped the powerful biceps with both hands and pushed his arm upward, propelling his blow harmlessly over her head. My own push, added to the momentum of his swing, spun him off balance helplessly, and when I let go, he spun around wildly a couple of times, like he was performing some weird tribal dance, before he toppled and fell heavily to the floor.

"Miss Russo," I said formally, "why don't you let me take you out of here to someplace where you can find civilized people?"

She smiled briefly, then shook her head. "I appreciate your offer, Mr. Holman, but Gino is right. We belong together. Without him I am nothing!"

I watched incredulously while she bent down, put her arm around his shoulders, then helped him back onto his feet with all the loving tenderness of a mother for her child. She murmured softly to him the whole time, and the liquid Italian had a sweet intimate sound. Amaldi allowed her to help him across the room and they slowly moved toward the front porch like reunited lovers fading happily into the sunset in the last few frames of the film.

"You look confused, Rick," Lenore said sweetly.

Her white teeth flashed at me in a sudden return of her old confidence.

"I would've figured about the last thing she needed right now was that bald-headed Svengali and his muscles!" I growled.

"You got a lot to learn about women, sonny-boy!" She chuckled derisively.

"I keep learning the whole time," I admitted, "and when it isn't fun, it sure is educational. It's been a real educational afternoon, come to think of it."

"What do you intend to do now, Mr. Holman?" Neilsen asked blandly.

"I was thinking of going straight home and maybe slashing my wrists in the bath," I said. "Even if I should change my mind, there will be no bill for services rendered, because there were no services rendered."

"I think we should talk," he said softly. "Lenore, I think you'd better get up onto the roadside and watch for the ambulance."

"But it couldn't possibly get here for another half hour at least," she objected.

"Then you'll be in good time to see it coming, my dear!"

She hesitated for a moment, then saw the expression on his face and didn't argue any more. The front door slammed shut behind her with unnecessary violence, and her heels clicked rapidly over the porch.

"Why don't you sit down, Mr. Holman?" Neilsen gestured toward the chair recently vacated by Carola Russo.

"I don't think so," I said curtly.

He smiled sadly at me, like I was one of the lambs that had strayed from the paths of righteousness. "You dislike me, Mr. Holman?"

"Doesn't everybody?" I snapped.

"I am a successful man in my way," he said, his rich bass voice counterpointing the words with a tonal modesty. "You are also a successful man in your own way. To maintain my success, I regret there are times when I have to be a pure son of a bitch. How about you, Mr. Holman?"

I grinned in spite of myself, then walked over to the chair and sat down. "So talk, Mr. Neilsen?" I said.

He lit a cigarette carefully, then studied my face for a few seconds before he spoke. "Rick—" He smiled "—you don't mind me calling you Rick?"

"It all goes on the bill," I said.

"I had an opportunity to speak with Gallant while the doctor was out of the room for a couple of minutes." He lowered his voice to make sure he wasn't overheard by either doctor or patient inside the bedroom. "Do you know exactly what happened out there?"

"Carola Russo told me about it."

"What do you make of it?"

"I haven't really thought about it," I said truthfully. "Right after she told me, Gallant staggered through the back door and all that blood was so dramatic, I gave it my full concentration."

He paced up and down slowly in front of me, his right hand sawing the air as he spoke. "I'd like you to think about it now, Rick. Carola came to the foot of the backstairs and called him. Gallant came to the door of the workshop. There was a shot, and the force of the bullet hitting him knocked him backwards into the workshop again. In the few seconds before he lost consciousness, he heard a second shot."

"Which smacked into the doorframe close to Carola as she was about to go to his help," I added. "Made her panic and run back up the stairs in here again. Not long after that, while she was still undecided what to do, she heard footsteps approaching from the road and Monica Hayes walked in—to kill her, Carola thought."

"But Monica didn't kill her," Neilsen said flatly. "You are the expert in these things, Rick, I would like to hear some of your expertise! What are the various possibilities arising out of those two shots?"

"An accident first," I said, and shrugged. "But unlikely. The world's worst shot couldn't accidentally place two bullets within a yard of each other! Then the obvious one—somebody tried to kill Gallant." I thought for a few seconds, then looked up sharply to meet the bland gaze of those mild blue eyes. "But then, why bother with a second shot when your first one already knocked him over? So there's another alternative— whoever it was wanted to kill them both, and the second shot was aimed at Carola."

"If you don't mind, Rick," he said apologetically, "I'd like to hear you say the last alternative?"

"That both shots were aimed at Carola Russo, but the first one went a little wide and Gallant was unlucky enough to be in the way?"

"Precisely!" He looked almost pleased. "I don't really believe for a moment that it was Monica Hayes. She doesn't have the guts for it in the first place; and if it was her, why didn't she kill Carola right here when they were alone together and she had every chance?"

"That makes sense," I admitted, "although somebody, especially a woman, with a gun in her hands often doesn't make sense. If they're motivated by some powerful emotion such as jealousy they can do the goddamnedest things! Monica could have fired those two shots meaning to kill both of them, and come in here ready to finish the job, then suddenly changed her mind for one of a million illogical reasons."

"I understand that!" There was a hint of impatience in his voice. "I'm not concerned with Monica Hayes primarily. It's Carola Russo who worries me. Someone tried to kill her this afternoon—I'm convinced of that! —and they may try again. I want you to find out who, and why, and stop them before they have a chance to try again, Rick!"

"That's quite an assignment," I said. "If you honestly think the girl's life is in danger, you should go to the police."

"How can I?" he rasped. "You heard me use a cheap dirty form of blackmail on Monica Hayes, to force her to keep quiet about this. If any of this leaks to the newspapers, Amaldi will quit the picture and take the girl straight back to Rome with him, and I would be ruined!"

The more I thought about it, the less I liked the whole idea, but I slowly realized I didn't have much choice. Like he'd just said, Neilsen would never tell the police he thought Carola Russo's life was in danger; and if I did, he'd have the others whipped into line to say it was only an accident when Gallant was cleaning his gun. I had to go along with it, maybe for Carola's sake if nothing else.

"There's another thing," Neilsen said in a musing voice. "I never like coincidence in the movies, even, and I detest it in real life. Yet, while Gallant and Carola are enjoying their temporary love nest up here—convinced they can safely do so for a few more days at least —Amaldi arrives back from Rome a week earlier than expected, and Monica also arrives back from her filming in the desert at least six days earlier than expected, too."

"You think they were tipped off?" I said.

"I think it's highly probable," he snapped. "I live and work in a specialized business where both emotions and money run high, Rick! They can make or break a man very quickly—overnight sometimes—if he ever makes the mistake of underestimating them. Let me particularize. Emotionally, both Monica and Gino Amaldi are very much involved. Amaldi is certainly capable of a murder for revenge, even if he has to hire an assassin to pull the trigger for him! Monetarily, my former partner, Sam Brunhoff, has never forgiven me for breaking away from Aria Productions to start my own company. The last time we spoke, he swore he'd ruin me, that I would never make this motion picture with Gallant and Carola Russo! A lot of Sam's financial backing comes from a man named Louis Martell— are you familiar with the name?"

"Some writer once called him 'one of the classic contradictions of our society,' I remember," I said, grinning. "Everybody knows he's been in the rackets for years, derives a very large income from the same source, and has probably been personally responsible for crimes ranging from assault to murder, but nobody's managed to come up with enough proof so far to even bring him into court."

"Then it wouldn't be any great strain for Martell to arrange a murder to help a business associate, and protect his own investments at the same time, would it?" Neilsen rasped.

"I guess not," I said, nodding. "If you think Amaldi's capable of killing the Russo girl, somebody had better keep a close eye on both of them."

"I'll take them out of their hotel on the way back," he said crisply. "They can stay at my house—Gino can't object when I tell him Carola's life may be in danger— and I can have them watched closely there."

"Fine," I said. "I wouldn't call this an easy one you've given me, Mr. Neilsen. It could take a long time—"

"Money is no object!" he said impatiently. "Remove the threat and name your own price, Rick!"

"I always do name my own price," I told him icily. "It so happens I wasn't thinking of money right now. I was thinking how I'd handle it, and maybe our ideas on the subject could differ."

"Differ?" He shot a sudden suspicious glance at me. "How differ? I want you to handle it the best way you know how, that's all! You're the expert—I said that before!"

"So you did," I acknowledged with no enthusiasm at all. "If I take this assignment, Mr. Neilsen, it's on condition you not only let me handle it my own way, but you don't squeal when people coming running to you with sore toes, either."

"Sore toes?"

"Sore, because I just stamped on them," I said.

"If my office is jammed full of sore toes every morning, I shall be completely unconcerned," he said easily.

"All I want from you is results, and I'm not interested how you get them. Is that clear, Rick?"

"That's fine," I agreed. "Then there's no need to keep you any longer."

I got up from the armchair and walked to the front door.

"Rick?" Neilsen said conversationally. "Doesn't the thought of tangling with Louis Martell make you nervous?"

"Not yet, anyway." I looked back over my shoulder at him. "What do you want? To sight my boy scout's badge of courage?"

"The thought did just occur to me that tangling with Martell could be dangerous, and if the alternative was to take a large sum of cash from him and keep quiet—?" He smiled beatifically. "What would you do, Rick?"

"You don't trust anyone, do you?" I said mildly.

"I've never had a good reason to, yet!"

"Not even Lenore Palmer?" I queried.

"Not even myself most days!"

I got the door open and stepped out onto the porch, then he spoke again in an almost jocular tone of voice.

"Incidentally, Rick, if you think you'll probably wind up in bed with Lenore during the next few days, you're almost certainly right. Only don't expect too much from the poor girl, will you? Since she got back from Rome, she just doesn't seem to have it any more. Do you think it could be the smog, maybe?"

I closed the door behind me and walked toward the road where Lenore Palmer stood listlessly in the heat of the afternoon, waiting for the ambulance that still couldn't possibly arrive for at least another fifteen minutes.

Maybe I had been wrong about Oscar Neilsen, I figured. He wasn't really a son of a bitch; more like a human vampire, the way he sank his fangs into people and never let go until he'd sucked them dry. I guessed it had one obvious advantage when it came the time to discard their husks; what little was left of a human being could be dropped down the kitchen sink, and neatly chewed to powder by the automatic garbage disposal unit.

chapter four

The easiest way to talk with a guy like Sam Brunhoff, I figured, was to go ring his doorbell and hope he was home. He wouldn't like it much, but I had learned to adjust to being one of the unloved during my formative years in senior high. For a couple of years then I had labored under the delusion that any girl I dated would reciprocate my own passionate desires for a definitely adult experience. I got to drink more ice cream sodas that way!

Home to Sam Brunhoff, I researched and discovered, was a sixth floor apartment in a very ostentatious new building on Sunset Boulevard. I arrived there around nine that evening and thumbed the doorbell hopefully.

"Come right on in, kids!" a bull-like voice roared from somewhere inside the apartment. "The door's open!"

So I went right in, through the spacious entrance hall, into the incredibly spacious living room, which had to rank high on the list of new wonders of the California world. It was the bachelor pad for the millionaire set, where money is only a word, but seduction can be a career. My feet sank in the gorgeously thick pile of white carpet, wall to wall; two giant-sized couches upholstered in a rich peacock-blue flanked one of the teak-paneled walls; a semicircular bar, stocked with enough booze to withstand twenty years of prohibition, protruded from the opposite wall.

There were a few minor details, of course, such as the push-button control panel set flush in the bartop, with each button neatly labeled. I couldn't resist pushing the one marked *Stereo* and almost immediately a soft rhythmic tango leaped out at me from a half-dozen different points in the room. The far wall was all plate glass, the drapes drawn back to reveal the myriad lights of Los Angeles obediently functioning as a kind of illuminated back lawn.

"You girls are kind of early," the bull-like voice rumbled in the entrance hall. "We're not even dressed yet, but I'll make you a drink to keep you company and—"

The voice's owner suddenly appeared in the doorway and stared blankly at me in surprise. He was built to match the sound of his voice, like an aging gorilla who could still go ten rounds with any of the young punks. His rapidly thinning brown hair was crew cut; his hooded brown eyes, set close together in his craggy face, were separated by a flattened nose that had been broken long before he'd joined the playboy set, I figured.

"Who the hell are you!" he bellowed at me, his fingers still automatically knotting his tie. "I thought it was the broads got here a little early—"

"I'm Rick Holman," I said and gave him a polite smile to go with the name. "You're Mr. Brunhoff?"

"Sure, I'm Sam Brunhoff! What the hell do you mean, busting in here like this!"

"I didn't bust in," I reminded him. "The door was open and you said to come inside."

"I thought you were the broads—" He shook his head

angrily. "We been through that already. Whatever it is you're peddling I don't want it, so get the hell out of here fast!"

"Oscar Neilsen figures you hate him so much, you wouldn't stop at murder, even," I said conversationally. "Is that right, Mr. Brunhoff?"

"What?" His jaw dropped and he gaped at me.

"Somebody took a couple of shots at the star of his new motion picture this afternoon," I added, "and right off, Oscar said who else could have organized it but that lousy son of a bitch, Sam Brunhoff!"

"Hey, Lou!" Brunhoff bellowed eagerly at the top of his thunderous voice. "Get in here real quick, boy, I got a live one going for me!"

The second man appeared through the doorway a few seconds later. His height and build were about average, but Brunhoff's bulk made him look small. The two of them would be around the same age, I figured, only the newcomer still had a full head of black hair, shot with gray. His eyes were a cold metallic blue, his face undistinguished, except for that slightly wooden expression which is often a cultivated asset for a professional gambler, or trial lawyer.

"Hey, Lou!" Brunhoff nudged him painfully with a sharp elbow jab. "Get this!" He speared a thick index finger toward me. "You! Say it again—all of it!"

So I said it again, all of it, and when I was finished, Brunhoff looked at the other guy with a gleeful expression on his face. "I told you I got a live one in here, didn't I? How do you like his style, busting right in here and giving me a spiel like that, huh? It's almost a shame I got to bust his nose and throw him out again, ain't it?"

"Sam," the smaller guy said in a thin, dried-up voice, "shut up, huh?"

"What did I say?" Brunhoff looked hurt.

The cold metallic blue eyes bored into my face for a long moment before he spoke again. "I am Louis Martell," he said finally. "Who are you?"

"Holman, he said," Brunhoff interjected happily. "Maybe he just came looking for a fight, Lou? He came to the right place. I haven't had a good fight in ten—"

"Sam?" The chill in Martell's voice stopped the bigger man as effectively as a gun butt. "Holman? I've heard that name before someplace." He thought for a few seconds. "Yeah, I remember now. He's the guy most studios take their big problems to, when they can't take 'em anyplace else except to the law, maybe."

"A kind of private detective, huh?" Brunhoff queried.

"He's got a fancy name for it, and fancy prices to match, I heard," Martell said.

Brunhoff took a deep anticipatory breath. "So I'll throw the bum out, anyway!"

"The way I heard it, this Holman has class," Martell said, "and, Sam? you never were the kind of fist-throwing moronic idiot you're playing now, so stop it, huh? Why do you suddenly want to be an actor, at your time of life?"

Brunhoff grinned briefly. "I don't know, the way he walked right in here and sounded off that way, it got me going somehow. Maybe the thought of that snake Oscar Neilsen being in back of it?"

"Okay, Mr. Holman," Martell said quietly. "I don't imagine you came here just to try and goad Sam into a fist fight?"

"I came here to find out if he's trying to murder one of Neilsen's stars," I said easily. "Maybe he got some professional advice from you, Mr. Martell, or you steered him to some friend of yours who was for hire?"

"Maybe Sam figures it's real cute the way you talk, Holman," he whispered, "but I don't."

"This shooting bit," Brunhoff said in a puzzled voice. "What is it? A rib, or something?"

"I don't think so." The small guy shook his head briefly. "I heard it on the radio tonight—Don Gallant accidentally shot himself in the shoulder early this afternoon, cleaning his gun while he was resting up in his cabin in the mountains—the radio said."

"Was he hurt bad?" Sam asked.

"Just a flesh wound." Louis Martell stared at me again. "So it wasn't an accident?"

"There were two shots," I told him. "Neilsen figures Gallant was just unlucky and got in the way of the first one. He figures both slugs were meant for Carola Russo."

"The Italian broad?" Sam shook his head ponderously. "I'm glad they missed, it would've been a tragic waste. There's a lot of mileage left in that sexy little tramp yet!"

"Sam is always a basic thinker in these things," Martell said vaguely. "Mr. Holman, obviously you're working for Neilsen in this, and he's told you one—or both —of us must be responsible for the shooting?"

"Right."

"Do you have an opinion of your own? Or is that something your employer wouldn't tolerate?"

"I'm not looking for an opinion," I said truthfully. "I want some facts. Neilsen says Sam Brunhoff has never forgiven him for breaking their partnership and starting his own company. He says Sam swore he'd ruin him, and see he never got to make this first picture with Carola Russo and Don Gallant. That's what Oscar Neilsen says. I'm curious to hear what Brunhoff and Martell say."

"Maybe we should have a drink?" Sam suggested, then glanced at his watch. "We got another half hour nearly, before the broads get here, Lou?"

"By all means let us have a drink," Martell said, nodding. Then something unnerving happened to the lower part of his face. For a horrible moment I thought the flesh was so stiff and dry, it had simply split; then, with a strong sense of relief, I realized he was smiling at me. "No reason we can't be friendly while we talk," he said. "What are you drinking, Rick?"

"Rye on the rocks would be fine, thanks, Lou," I said.

"I'll get them," Brunhoff announced. "Your usual, Lou?"

I sat beside Martell on a shining, stainless-steel bar-stool, while Brunhoff played bartender in front of us.

"Sam and Oscar Neilsen were partners in Aria Productions," Lou said casually. "About four years back, Neilsen figured they could make a fortune out of foreign production if they only had the money to back it. He made a real good pitch, and when Sam told me the story, I figured it looked good, too. So I loaned him a hundred grand, and put in a couple of hundred of my own. Neilsen took off and spent the next four years in Rome, only coming back here for a trip maybe a couple of times every year."

"He made movies over there, okay!" Sam snorted. "Only the movies he made didn't make any money! And things weren't so goddamned good here, either. Our market always was the second feature, but it's being steadily squeezed right out of the business. So what with us losing money here, and Oscar losing money over there, things looked bad. Then one bright morning around six months back, Oscar flies in from Rome with a big deal that just can't fail to get back all the money we've lost already, and a hell of a lot more besides!"

Lou Martell put down his glass carefully onto the bartop and looked at me with a brooding expression in his eyes.

"With costs the way they are in the industry these days," he said almost pedantically, "you understand, Rick, to achieve a successful top quality motion picture—which means you got to spend at least eight million!—is like making a five-horse parlay. You start with a property like a best-seller book, and that maybe gets you a big-name star, which gets you a top director—and that kind of combination will get you finance from the bank, or the guys who want to distribute your picture."

"That's what Oscar had," Sam said gloomily. "A parlay! He told us he'd gotten the rights to a classy best-seller in Europe, written by some French guy; the big Italian star, Carola Russo, was crazy to do the film, but Gino Amaldi handled all her business, and he wouldn't sign unless Oscar had gotten a big-name American star to play opposite the broad."

"This Amaldi is a smart punk," Lou grunted. "He figures his broad can really act, but her name won't mean nothing over here, so if a big American name plays opposite her it'll mean box office here."

"Oscar keeps his best news until last," Brunhoff snarled. "He knows Don Gallant is crazy to make a movie with the Italian broad, ever since he met her in Europe last year. All he needs is fifty thousand to keep Gallant's agent happy, he says, and we got the whole deal wrapped up tight!"

"It sounded good," Lou said gently, "real good. So we dig up the fifty thousand. It's only when Oscar tells us he's decided to quit, and we can take the fifty grand out of his half share of the assets—what goddamned assets?—do we find out that the whole parlay belongs to him. He's set up Cadenza and signed *personal* contracts with the writer, the Italian broad, and Gallant! With all that clutched in his hand, he's got to fight off the people who want to finance him with a club!"

"So Oscar Neilsen is a lousy fink, and a stinking son of a bitch!" Sam growled. "And maybe I do say a lot of hard things at the time, and mean them! But trying to blow holes in lover-boy Gallant—?"

"Is absurd, of course," Martell said. "We'll fix that double-crossing creep's wagon but good! Only legitimately, within the industry itself."

"So maybe it takes a little time." Brunhoff smiled nastily. "We can wait!"

I finished my drink and put the glass down on the bartop beside Lou's, then slid off the stool.

"Thanks for the drink, and your time," I said politely. "I appreciate all your troubles, gentlemen, and you telling me about them."

"Maybe you do have an opinion now, Rick?" Martell asked in an indifferent-sounding voice.

"About what?"

"Don't get cute about it, punk!" he hissed. "Anything I can't stand, it's somebody getting cute with me."

"Take it easy, Lou." Brunhoff grinned broadly at me, but his eyes were coldly calculating. "What Lou means is, now you heard our side of the story, maybe you don't believe Neilsen's version any more?"

"I think maybe the truth is about halfway between the two," I said truthfully. "If you want my honest opinion on something else, I'd say you were a pretty good actor, anyway, Sam. And Lou makes one of the best straight men in the business. The way you both put that act over was real cute. I could almost believe it *would* be ridiculous to think either of you had anything to do with the shooting, if I could forget Lou's intimate association with the rackets goes back over twenty years!"

They looked at each other for a moment in silence, then Brunhoff shook his head regretfully. "I should have thrown the bum out of here in the first place!" He lumbered around the end of the bar and started toward me purposefully.

"You don't have to do that, Sam," I told him. "I'm leaving, anyway."

"It's no trouble" he said, smiling blissfully. "I'll enjoy it!"

When he was close enough, he threw a haymaking right at my face which would have separated my head from my shoulders if it had connected. I ducked inside it and slammed the stiffened fingers of my right hand into his stomach. They sank deep into the fatty tissue, and he made a shrill whistling sound like it was time for the graveyard shift to start work. I backed off a little as he glared bloody murder at me, his face a dirty gray color, and swung at me again. This time I grabbed his wrist, about-faced, and pulled hard on it as I bent forward at the same time. He came up over my shoulder into a brief, spectacular orbit that ended abruptly when he hit the floor on his back, with a thud that must have shaken the whole building.

After a little while, when he'd gotten some air back into his lungs, he glared up at me with a bewildered expression on his face. "How in hell did that happen?" he gurgled thickly.

"I don't know." I looked down at him for a moment, then shook my head sadly. "I guess you just don't live right, Sam!"

I walked out of the apartment, not forgetting to close the front door behind me gently, then lit a cigarette while I waited for the elevator. When it finally arrived two girls got out, who were far too busy talking and giggling at each other to even notice me. One was a bouncy little blonde with a beehive hairdo who looked like she'd been hothouse bred for penthouse purposes. The other girl was taller, with dark brown hair and a pixie face; she had a lot more class than the bouncy little blonde. They walked slowly toward the door of Brunhoff's apartment, still giggling furiously at each other.

I pressed the button to hold the elevator doors open, then said, "Hey! Does this come under the heading of more judicious experience for a twenty-three-year-old?"

They both stopped and turned their heads toward me, with the usual look of outraged indignation on their faces.

"Well, really!" the bouncy little blonde said in an impossibly refined voice. "A girl just isn't safe anywhere these days!"

The brown-haired girl didn't say anything. A look of dismayed recognition showed in her hazel eyes, then she bit down savagely on her lower lip.

"Ah, there, Janie!" I said politely, then let the elevator door slowly wipe them from my view.

chapter five

The morning sun demonstrated its strict impartiality by casting the same brilliant heat down on Oscar Neilsen's house in the Palisades as it did on the rest of the world. I parked the car on the raked driveway in front of the house, then walked up onto the front porch and rang the doorbell. When I called him earlier and asked could he fix it for me to talk with Carola Russo, he'd agreed to take Amaldi with him downtown and keep him busy until early afternoon anyway, so I wouldn't have to fight off the little fat man the whole time I was trying to talk to the girl.

A tall, lean, sinewy-looking character opened the front door and stared at me impassively. His thick black hair was neatly slicked down with a pomade that smelled a little too rich for my blood, and his swarthy face was devoid of expression, to match his dark eyes. One quick look and I figured he had to be something between an undertaker's mute and a sales representativ from the Mafia.

"My name's Holman," I said. "I—"

"You're expected, Mr. Holman," he said in a flat voice. "I'm Tino—the houseman."

"Fine," I said vaguely. "Is Miss Russo—?"

"She's out by the pool in back of the house," he interrupted again. "Would you like me to bring you some refreshments in a while, Mr. Holman?"

"That sounds great." I checked my watch and saw it was after eleven, anyway. "A martini would be a friendly gesture, an eight-to-one mix—"

"And mind I don't bruise the gin?" He smiled wearily.

I looked at him for a moment, then gave him the weary smile right back. "I always did think that one was cute," I admitted. "And I don't know what Miss Russo drinks, but—"

"Vodka tonic," he said blandly, "and the ice has to be in cubes, not cracked."

"I bet Mr. Neilsen trained you personally," I said confidently. "You have exactly the same kind of repulsive efficiency, Tino."

"Thank you." His eyes sneered at me for a moment. "Is there anything else I can do for you?"

"I guess I can find the back of the house all by myself," I said. "You don't have any mad dogs running loose in the grounds, by any chance?"

"Not since I came here." He smiled—or his thin lips twisted a little, anyway. "I made them unnecessary."

"Let me know the next time you're about to run loose in the grounds," I suggested. "That's something I'd like to see!"

"Would you like some Girl Scout homebaked cookies, along with the drinks, Mr. Holman?" He shrugged gently. "I wouldn't want you to run out of steam halfway through the morning."

I turned away from the open door with a look of respect on my face. "I guess if they had known a new breed of housemen was coming," I said over my shoulder, "they would have started building bigger houses?"

A few seconds later I found the pool was right there in back of the house like he'd promised. Carola Russo was stretched out on her back beside it, adding another coat of tan to her body which was already toasted a nice warm brown. I stopped maybe two feet away from her and looked down. She wore a black cotton bikini, which was about the barest concession to propriety she could make. One thin strip straddled her hips firmly, while the other fought hopelessly to contain the thrust of her high tilted breasts.

If you analyzed it, I told myself, she was just a girl— a girl with long slender legs, boyish hips, and a disproportionately big bosom. So why, I asked myself weakly, did I get this almost uncontrollable aching desire every time I looked at her? There was no answer, of course. How the hell can anyone define the indefinable?—that magic plus in sex appeal maybe only one girl in a hundred thousand is born with?

Some natural built-in radar warning system told her yet another predatory male was too close for comfort, and her eyes opened wide. I stared down into their jade-green depths, and suddenly found myself back in the jungle again. Only this time it was peaceful and shone with a tropical brilliance, undisturbed by any trace of the implacable hunter.

"Mr. Holman?" She sat up slowly and stretched her arms over her head in a luxuriant movement that almost lifted her breasts straight out of the bikini top. "What are you doing here?"

"I wanted to talk a little with you, Miss Russo," I said in a slightly ragged voice. "I hope I didn't disturb you?"

"No." She looked into my eyes and suddenly let her arms drop back to her sides. "But I'm disturbing you, huh?"

"It's part of your fate to disturb all men, Miss Russo," I said. "Maybe you can't help it, but neither can the men."

"You're just giving me facts, so you won't have to apologize!" She gave me a gamin grin, then held out her hands toward me. "Help me up, please."

I pulled her onto her feet and there was only the lightest resistance from her body weight. She walked toward a table and two chairs set in the shade of a tree. I followed her, unable to take my eyes away from the view of her small rounded buttocks gently swaying in front of me. By the time we sat down, my whole body ached with a quivering frustrated tension.

"You want to talk about the shooting yesterday afternoon?" she said with an obvious reluctance. "Mr. Neilsen explained everything later on—that's why we moved out of the hotel and came here."

The figure of Tino appeared outside the back of the house, and came toward us carrying a tray.

"Good!" The girl clapped her hands like a small child. "Just what I need right now!"

The houseman circled the pool, then came up to the table and lowered the tray carefully onto it. As he straightened up, his arm accidentally brushed against her shoulder and he stiffened for a moment, a sudden gleam in his dark eyes. If it was any consolation it proved me right about her having the same effect on all men, I figured sourly.

"Is there anything else I can bring you, Miss Russo?" Tino asked politely.

"No." She picked up the long vodka tonic and looked at it gloatingly. "That's lovely, thank you."

"How about you, Mr. Holman?" His voice changed subtly, so what had been polite respect to Carola Russo, became insolent contempt for me.

"I'll be perfectly content if you just disappear, Tino," I smiled warmly at him. "Frankly, you're spoiling the view!"

He stood without moving for a brief moment, then nodded, veiling the momentary spark of fury that had showed in his eyes. Then he walked away noiselessly, lithe on his feet like a cat.

"Do you always treat servants like that?" Carola Russo asked coldly.

"Only that one," I said. "He's special, and it's a kind of private joke between the two of us, anyway."

"Oh?" She shrugged her bare shoulders easily. "Then you're forgiven." She lifted her glass. "Here's to the pallbearers!"

"Miss Russo," I said. "I——"

"Make it Carola." She lowered her glass and looked at me impatiently. "What's got into you this morning? You were much nicer yesterday afternoon, trying to save me from Gino——although I had it coming, anyway!"

"I guess I had a bunch of other things to worry about then." I said truthfully. "This morning there's only you around, and it makes me a little nervous."

Her mouth set in a sullen pout: "It drives you crazy, just looking at me?" A bored expression showed on her face. "Don't bother with the rest of the routine. Mr. Holman, I know it off by heart and the answer's still no!"

"Even in a television western, the heroine has the same effect on both the goodies and the baddies!" I snarled. "But you can always tell the goodies——they're the ones who keep their hands off!"

She giggled, and spilled some of her drink down the front of herself. I watched the glistening drops of vodka tonic trickle down the deep division between her breasts for a moment, and it almost made me an instantaneous baddy.

"I'm sorry," she gurgled. "It's gotten to be a kind of automatic reflex with me, Mr.——it's Rick, isn't it?"

"It's Rick," I agreed. "And I don't seem to be getting anyplace. Neilsen hired me to find out who fired those shots and to stop them firing any more, and I had a sense of urgency about the whole deal right up until I met you again."

"I didn't want to spoil a beautiful morning by talking about it, Rick," she said softly. "But you're right, we have to talk about it, although I don't know how I can help at all. You ask me all the questions you want, and I promise to be a good little girl and answer them for you!"

"What were you doing in Rome when Gino Amaldi discovered you, Carola?" I asked.

Her face froze. "What's that got to do with people shooting at me?"

"You promised you'd be a good little girl, remember?" I snapped.

"Yes, I did promise, didn't I?" She returned the empty glass to the tray, relaxed in the chair, and ran her fingers slowly through her tousled red hair. "What was I doing in Rome when Gino found me?" she repeated the words slowly to herself.

"I was trying to stay alive so I'd still be around when the big break came my way, mainly. There are various ways a girl can do this on the Via Veneto, and they're all unpleasant. I know because I did them all."

Her jade-green eyes stared bleakly into the distance. "The first time I met Gino was in a hotel bedroom where he was waiting for a call girl to show up. I was a little late, so he backhanded me across the face for it, almost before I'd gotten inside the door. But after that first time his genius recognized my talents, so he always asked for me whenever he contacted the call girl service."

"Carola," I said gently, "you don't have to—"

"Now I've started, let me finish it!" she said bitterly. "My big break came one night when he didn't have the money to pay me, and couldn't stand the thought of me walking out on him. He made a deal, I could play a walk-on part the next day in the film he was making then, and it would be worth a little more than my usual rates for the usual services I normally rendered. I thought it sounded all right, so I did it. A couple of days later he called me to meet him that afternoon at the studio. When I got there he showed me the scene I'd played and said I was a lot more sexy on the screen than I'd ever been in a hotel bedroom.

"I thought he wanted to cheapen the price and started screaming at him."

She laughed: the harsh sound mocked the brilliant sunlight, dirtied the sparkling blue water that rippled in the pool. "What Poppa Gino meant, of course, was he'd suddenly realized I had something he didn't need to buy any more, because he could sell it! I signed a contract with him the same afternoon, which improved my life immensely—from being a would-be starlet and paid whore, I became a paid starlet and an unpaid mistress!

"Gino taught me how to act and I learned fast, because he always used his heavy hands on me to point up a mistake! He invented a wonderful campaign of torture for me, made up of diets to slim me down, physical exercises, massage, and diets to fatten me up again—until he'd gotten an extra two inches onto my bust and three inches off my hips. The top-heavy look, he called it. 'A woman from the waist up and a boy from the waist down. Like this, *cara,* you appeal to every taste!' And he was right, we became a big success, Rick. Isn't that nice?"

She sat up straight and looked at me, her face set in a mask of naked bitterness. "What's the matter, Rick? I thought everybody likes hearing a success story because it always makes them feel good?"

"I couldn't stand any more, Carola baby," I said softly. "It would make me bust out crying!"

"You think I made it up?" She spat the words at me with a cold contempt.

"No—" I shook my head. "I believe every word you said."

"And it amuses you?"

"It amuses me," I agreed. "Not the story—*you!*"

"*Me!*"

"You're so goddamned arrogant," I told her. "Self-pity is about the greatest form of arrogance there is. You sit there telling me your big success story, and you're wallowing up to your neck in self-pity the whole time! Poor little Carola, the lonely, unprotected little girl who was prepared to do anything to become a big star. So she was made to do everything she was prepared to do—and she became a big star!"

I slumped back into my chair. "I don't see anything tough about that. If you hadn't made it in the end, it might be different. If you told me they fished your pathetic little body out of the Tiber one night, after Amaldi had gotten you with child and thrown you back onto the streets—then I would bust out crying!"

Her jade-green eyes froze into icicles of pure hate, as the color drained completely from her tortured face. Then her mouth dropped open and she screamed. The thin sound was pitched on one constant, nerve-strumming note of raw agony—the moment before she leaped at me with the cold-blooded ferocity of a beast from the jungle.

Both hands clawed for my face, the long nails savagely raking toward my skin. I managed to grab her wrists as the sudden impact of her body tilted the chair sideways, so we fell to the ground and rolled over and over across the grass while she still fought like a wildcat. Finally we came to a stop with her heaving body underneath mine. I slowly forced her wrists back onto the grass at either side of her head, and sat heavily on her bare midriff. She still struggled violently for a few seconds more, then closed her eyes and let her body go limp.

"You got to grow up emotionally sometime, baby!" I grated breathlessly. "You and Poppa Gino were a mutual arrangement—you used him just as much as he used you!"

She opened her eyes and glared up at me. "What are you going to do now, Professor Freud Holman? Rape me—to prove a point?"

I let go her wrists and got up onto my feet. She rolled over onto her side away from me, so I couldn't see her face while I lit a cigarette.

"Go away, drop dead!" she said in a muffled voice. "You're loathsome!"

"When Poppa Gino left you here alone and went back to Rome," I snarled at her, "you couldn't wait to get into that mountain shack with Gallant! Then yesterday when Poppa Gino caught you red-handed, you wouldn't let me stop him from slugging you. A mutual arrangement, baby! You had your kicks with Gallant, so you were determined to get your lumps from Amaldi. It's known as guilt transference; just so long as you can blame him for everything—and believe it!— you can keep right on wallowing in all that saccharine self-pity!"

"Leave me alone!" she whimpered hysterically. "You've got a mind like a sewer!"

"Time is running out fast for you, baby," I said softly. "If you stop and listen hard a moment, you'll hear it."

"I won't listen, you hear!" she said in a thin, childish wail. "Leave me alone!"

"I know, and you know, baby, how you feel toward Amaldi," I snarled. "But who knows how he feels toward you? How does a little fat man with a shining bald head feel toward a beautiful actress he's made into a sex symbol famous throughout the world? What does life hold for him in a future without you? Does he think that your little episode with Gallant is the beginning of the end for him? That sooner or later, one of the good-looking young men will take you away from him forever?"

"You're crazy!" she moaned.

"Sitting high in the clouds on his way back from Rome," I went on, "did Poppa Gino come to a decision? Did he decide that, rather than lose you to a younger man, he would prefer you were dead? So then you would always be his creation entirely, from birth to death?" I paused for a couple of moments. "The jackpot question, baby! Was the finger that pulled the trigger paid for by Poppa Gino?"

Carola pulled herself up into a sitting position, then turned her head toward me in a slow, painful movement. The look on her face cried out for pity, but I was convinced right then that pity was the one sure way to destroy her completely.

"You don't understand Poppa Gino," she said in a brittle voice. "Because to you he looks a funny little man, you think he must look that way to everyone else, including himself! You don't know me, either, if you think I spent those four miserable days in that stinking cabin with Gallant just for kicks!"

"I know you, baby!" I said icily. "Every time I look into those jade-green eyes of yours, I know you! Your whole world is mirrored in your eyes, did you know that?"

"What world?" she sneered.

"A world of fear, baby," I whispered. "A jade-green jungle that's alive with brilliant colors and dark shadows where the wild beasts roam. But they don't worry you, because it's your world and you've learned to survive in it. Only now a new factor has been added, and it means your only hope of survival is to leave the jungle, but you don't know how."

"What new factor?" In spite of herself, she couldn't resist asking the question.

"The hunter," I said. "The wild beasts prey on each other looking for an easy kill, and if you're careful in the jungle you can easily keep out of their way. But the hunter is different, he follows his destiny and stalks only his predestined prey—which is you!"

"One look into my eyes and you can see all that?" She laughed contemptuously. "You're out of your mind!"

"Maybe." I shrugged. "Aren't you already about halfway out of yours?"

She climbed onto her feet and wrapped her arms tight around her body, shivering slightly in spite of the sun's brilliant heat. "What do you want from me, Rick Holman?" There was the sound of despair in her voice.

"For you to tell me if the hunter's name is Gino Amaldi," I said truthfully.

"Gino is the last man in the world who would want to see me dead," she said flatly. "Now I've answered your question, will you leave me alone?"

"Yes," I said.

She turned and walked away from me, her body still shivering spasmodically. I stood there and watched until she finally disappeared inside the house. Then I too shivered slightly in spite of the sun's brilliant heat.

chapter six

It was about the first time I had ever seen a white uniform wiggle, I realized, as I followed the nurse up the stairs in Gallant's house. Lenore Palmer had obviously taken Neilsen's instructions to heart the previous afternoon, because this was without doubt the sexiest nurse I had ever seen in my whole life.

She stopped outside the bedroom door and looked at me with that air of furtive conspiracy, so beloved by the medical profession whenever they discuss a patient with an outsider. My guess is the nurses started it, then the doctors took it over, and they finally gave it to the morticians. It always makes my flesh crawl.

"I won't go in with you, Mr. Holman," the nurse whispered confidentially. She took time out to caress briefly her silver blond hairdo.

"I'll just wait downstairs until you're through."

"Thank you," I grunted.

She batted her eyelashes a couple of times, as if to strengthen our unspoken conspiracy against her patient.

"I'm sure there's no need to remind you, Mr. Holman, but you won't stay too long, will you? I won't like you, if you leave him exhausted!"

"I bet you always leave him that way, Nurse!" I said, matching her confidential whisper.

Her mouth opened a full half-inch, then the lower lip protruded in a carefully calculated pout. "Why, Mr. Holman!" She giggled archly. "I don't know what you mean!"

"If I could only bet on that, honey," I said, sighing heavily, "we'd have a date for lunch and dinner every day for the next six weeks. Oh, you kid!"

Then I pushed open the door and stepped quickly into the bedroom in case she decided to accept the offer.

Don Gallant was sitting up in bed, his back propped comfortably against a stack of cushions, earnestly watching a soap opera on daytime television. The box office appeal, which created his asking price of a quarter-million dollars, hit you right between the eyes the moment you looked at him, I grudgingly admitted to myself—the crisp, curly black hair, the long melancholy face with a determined jawline and firm mouth, and the clear skin tanned to a rich mahogany color.

The clean white bandage across his shoulder was definitely the final deft stroke of an artist's brush. One look at that and you just knew instinctively this was the hero who got it over Pusan yesterday after he'd shot down twenty-eight Migs while nursing the tattered remnants of his squadron back to base.

"Mr. Gallant?" I pitched my voice loud enough to override the soap opera's heroine, who was passionately pleading with her husband to give her lover an even break, for the sake of the children.

He pressed the remote-control button and a moment later both picture and sound died a simultaneous death. Then he studied the blank screen with a brooding expression stamped on his fine-chiseled face. (*Dialogue: "I tell you, Captain, it means certain death for the man that attempts this mission!" Gallant, smiling wryly: "I know, Colonel, that's why I'm going myself!"*)

"You know," Gallant said slowly, a brooding tone in his voice to match the look on his face. "I just don't understand what people see in television."

"You mean," I said cleverly, "it doesn't compare with the movies?"

"I suppose I do!" He looked pleased with himself. "And it's all so—well—so phony!"

"You're absolutely right," I agreed. "When you compare it with any movie—the last one of yours I saw, for example? What was it called again? Something about 'The Sultan—' ?"

" '—and the Slavegirl!' " he said quickly. "Thank you, Holman. It so happens I wholeheartedly agree with you. Those sets were authentic Egyptian, right down to the last detail, you know?"

"I thought it was meant to an Arabian background?"

"It happened to be an historical motion picture," he said coldly. "Back in those days, Arabia and Egypt were practically the same thing, anyway! Wardrobe spent over fifty thousand dollars on Yvonne Clavel's costumes, alone."

"I never realized she was wearing costumes," I said, genuinely impressed. "I thought she just ran around in her underwear all through the picture."

Gallant refused to answer that; instead he gave me a long hard stare from under his crisp black eyebrows, and after a while it made me feel nervous. (*Dialogue: "Okay, Holman, if there just ain't any other way of proving I'm the law in these parts—draw!"*)

"How's the shoulder today?" I said, for a change of subject matter.

"Fine!" He winced sharply and closed his eyes as he slumped back against the cushions. "Just fine," he added, from between clenched teeth. He waited until the timing was right, then grinned manfully. "The doctor says I lost somewhere close to a couple of pints of good red blood." He made it a throwaway line.

"You must have one hell of a constitution!" I said in an admiring voice.

"I keep in shape." He smiled modestly, revealing a row of teeth that had been capped by an artist. "I never use a stuntman, you know, Holman? That can make it pretty rugged at times!"

"About that shooting yesterday afternoon," I said determinedly. "I—"

"It was an accident," he snapped. "Some moron with no gun-sense probably aimed at a sitting bird and potted me instead!"

"The second shot only missed Carola Russo by inches," I reminded him.

"Ah!" He gave me a knowing smile. "For a moment I almost forgot just how you earn a living, Holman! It's to your advantage to try and make something out of this, of course. But I'm afraid you'll have to do it without any help from me, old boy!"

"It's Oscar Neilsen's idea in the first place, not mine," I grated. "He figures somebody was out to kill Carola Russo, and you got hit by mistake."

"Mistake?" His eyes goggled at the sheer effrontery of the thought. "That's ridiculous!"

"Anyway"—it was my turn to give him a knowing smile—"I guess it was worth it, accident or not, for those four glorious days with Carola, huh?"

His face clouded darkly as he scowled at me for a moment. "Gallant by name, and gallant by nature, that's me!" He paused uncertainly when I didn't react. "That's a joke! But I have to confess Carola Russo was a bitter disappointment to me. When it comes down to the real action, the girl is as sexy as my great-aunt Mathilda— and I do mean the one who's eighty-five next birthday and still thinks that 'sex' is the one that comes next after 'five'! I have never endured a greater period of sheer monotony than those four days in the cabin!"

"You don't tell me?" I said respectfully.

"Imagine how any normal girl would react in this situation, Holman?" he said bitterly. "It's night on the mountainside, but inside the log cabin everything is snug and warm. In front of her an open fire burns brightly, the logs crackling, and there's a smell of pinewood in the room. She sits comfortably on the white lamb's-wool rug, occasionally sipping fine liquor from a genuine antique Spanish goblet, watching the fire-light's glow—and beside her is—well—me!"

"I can imagine," I agreed. "How did the Russo girl react?"

"She yawned!" His voice quivered with indignation. "When I slid my arm around her shoulders and mur-mured some of those intimate little terms of endearment a girl likes to hear, she clicked her teeth!" He closed his eyes again as an even more painful memory re-turned: "My God!" he suddenly yelped. "That girl must be one of the great romantics of all time! Later, I cupped my hand under her chin and gently turned her face toward mine to kiss her, and you know what she said? 'Skip the corny preliminaries, friend, and get to the main event—I'm tired and I need a good night's sleep!' *That's* what she said!"

"It's hardly the language of love," I said sympathet-ically.

"That's another thing!" he muttered. "Her language would make a stevedore blush! No, you can take it from me, that Russo girl is one big fake, and that's why the thought of anybody getting passionate enough about her to the point of murder, is completely absurd!"

"I'll take your word for it," I said. "How's your wife?"

"Please!" He shuddered violently. "Don't use that dirty word, Holman!"

"You don't think she felt passionate enough about the situation to go after you with a gun?"

"Monica?" He laughed mirthlessly. " Let me tell you about Monica! Her aggressive neurosis is based entirely on a strong sense of inferiority, and that of course makes for all her traumatic lapses into morbidity, hysteria, and occasional psychosis!"

"You mean she's jealous of you?" I said.

"Yes—" he blinked slowly a couple of times "—I guess that's exactly what I mean! But she's also convinced her husband is the best status symbol she's ever owned, so she wouldn't rob herself of that, whatever the provocation!" He smiled with smug satisfaction at his own image reflected in the blank television screen. "Monica knows that I'm the best thing she's ever had in her whole life! Confidentially, Holman, she freely acknowledges the fact in bed. All the bitchiness starts once she gets her feet back onto the floor!"

About then I figured I'd suffered all the intimate confessions of the great lover I could stand in one day. "Well, it's been real nice visiting with you, Mr. Gallant," I said. "I hope the shoulder heals quickly."

"It will," he said complacently. "Nice of you to drop around and see me, Holman." A nasty little smile played around the corners of his mouth for a few moments. "Sorry I can't help you dream up a big murder plot impressive enough to squeeze a nice fat fee out of Oscar Neilsen—but then, I never was much good at conniving, I'm afraid!"

"You want me to send the nurse back in here?" I asked coldly.

"No!" His face paled slightly. "I wish Monica would get home so I can tell her that nurse has got to go! Under that white uniform lurks a sex maniac, Holman! I'm too scared to take a nap, even, while she's around, in case she's right there under the covers with me when I wake up!"

"Have you talked with your psychiatrist lately?" I queried.

"Not in the last couple of months since—" He stopped suddenly and flashed a suspicious glance at my face. "Why? What made you ask that question?"

"It's probably nothing," I said in a soothing voice, as I headed toward the door. "Nothing at all to worry about, anyway."

"*What* is nothing to worry about?" he yelled.

"It's only that sometimes all these sexual fantasies, like the ones you're having, are a kind of warning that there is a real physical problem," I said vaguely. "But I wouldn't worry about it."

His head reared up from the cushions: "What kind of a real physical problem?"

"Well—" I opened the door and stepped out into the hallway, before I looked back at his haggard face. "Loss of virility, actually." I smiled warmly. "But that's obviously absurd in your case! I mean, you haven't noticed in recent weeks that there's been any lack of response from women toward you, for example? The old magic's working the same as it ever did, right?"

"Oh, my God!" He fell back onto the cushions, his face a pallid gray beneath the tan. "Those four days in the cabin!" There was an undertone of tragic irony in his voice, "I suppose it's amusing in a macabre kind of way? All this time I've believed that *she* was the sexless one!"

"It's not the kind of thing you want to get around," I suggested, and he quivered at the thought. "Nurses have a sharp nose for that kind of thing," I went on. "It's only a suggestion, but why don't you pretend to make a big play for her—then she'll never suspect?"

"Thanks, old buddy!" He smiled gratefully. "I'll have her convinced she's the hottest thing in my life since puberty, inside the next thirty minutes!"

I closed the door behind me and walked slowly along the hallway, figuring that by the time I'd finished with him, that son of a bitch would think twice about using a word like "conniving" to me again. The nurse reached the top of the stairs at the same time I did, and stopped for another intimate chat.

"And how did you find Mr. Gallant today?" she asked brightly.

I looked her up and down a couple of times, not missing a thing, then shook my head in open admiration.

"That Don!" I said. "He sure has good taste."

"You mean he has good taste in nurses, Mr. Holman?" she giggled hopefully.

"I mean he sure can pick them." I explained. "Pick the ones with a big movie potential, I mean." I had to talk that way to pound the idea through her thick skull. "You know something? He's already half-talked me into giving you a small featured role in his next picture!"

"Me?" She glowed warmly as her face lit up like a Christmas candle. "You mean, Mr. Gallant wants me to have a part in his next movie?"

"Look, honey"—I dropped my voice to a whisper— "I wouldn't want anybody to hear me say this right out loud, but he's crazy for you. He's flipped! The big trouble is, he says, you obviously just don't care for him at all."

"That's just not true!" she said passionately. "I think Mr.—Don!—is just about the most attractive man I ever met in my whole life!"

"Then a smart girl like you should let him know how you feel, honey," I told her. "Why don't you give him some real personal attention?" I gave her substantial bosom a gentle nudge with my elbow. "Know what I mean?"

Her lower lip protruded almost to the point of no return, while a slow deep breath helped her absorb the idea and give her pectoral muscles a workout at the same time.

"Mr. Holman," she said in a hushed, dedicated voice, "I think I know exactly what you mean!"

I watched her ecstatic wiggle as she trotted toward Gallant's room, and felt the warm glow deep inside that comes with the sense of a mission accomplished. *Conniving* yet!

It was around five-thirty when I parked outside that brand-new building on Wilshire Boulevard and went looking for Oscar Neilsen. The boss had gone home already, I discovered about five minutes later, and had taken Gino Amaldi with him. So I went up to the fourth floor to see if some of the hired help were still around.

The public relations director was busy pecking away at a typewriter on her desk, and had taken off the coat of her brown linen suit to get right down to it. That left her in a sleeveless white silk blouse, and me in a state of stunned admiration. Her office door was open when I arrived, so I just leaned against the frame and watched. Every time she breathed, the white silk flattened against the thrust of her full breasts—fluttered gently—then flattened again. Somehow, being a Peeping Tom in office hours didn't seem so bad. I didn't feel like a voyeur, or anything the head shrinkers could get their teeth stuck into, anyway.

After a couple of minutes she lifted her head, and her luminous blue eyes widened a fraction. "Well! How long have you been standing there?"

"Long enough to admire the view," I admitted. "Did you know that silk blouse is sexy?"

"Everything I wear is sexy," she said complacently. "I'm sexy! I'm about the sexiest public relations director in the business. Didn't you know that?"

I walked a little further into her office and dropped into the armchair shaped like an eggeshell. "I really came around to see your boss, but he's gone home."

"I don't like the way you say that!" Her wide mouth quirked suddenly. "You make it sound like my boss is even sexier than I am."

"I was out at his house this morning." I stopped for a moment to light a cigarette. "It looked like a nice house."

"It is," she said, nodding. "Very impressive!"

"I found the houseman even more impressive than the house," I admitted. "Where did Neilsen ever find him?"

"Tino?" She smiled. He is quite something, isn't he! Mr. Neilsen decided he needed a personal assistant sometime during our last year in Europe, and he picked up Tino while he was back here on a trip."

"From personal assistant to houseman?" I raised my eyebrows. "That's quite a fall, isn't it?"

"I imagine it was Tino himself who said he was the houseman?" She looked faintly amused, "It would be his idea of a joke. He has a strange sense of humor."

"I was impressed," I said idly. "Neilsen couldn't have had much time to shop around if he was only here on a trip. How did he manage to pick up a personal assistant like Tino in so short a time?"

"That was back in the Aria Productions days, of course," Lenore remembered. "He asked his partner to find him somebody he could trust, and I think it was Louis Martell who recommended Tino? Something like that, anyway."

"I had a friendly talk with Brunhoff and Martell last night," I said.

"I didn't know it was possible to have a friendly talk with those two crooks?" she said coldly.

"The way they tell it, it was old saintly Oscar who double-crossed them, and lifted the whole Carola Russo-Don Gallant deal, right from under their noses!"

Her face reddened slightly. "Mr. Neilsen worked his heart out those four years in Europe! But those bastards never gave him any support at all! If they couldn't get a theatrical release over here for the pictures he made, they could have gotten a television deal if they'd only half-tried! They broke his heart for him, Rick."

"Oscar Neilsen has a heart?" I grinned widely. "You've got to be kidding!"

"It's just that you don't—or won't!—understand him," she said hotly. "I know he likes to make himself sound like the typical son-of-a-bitch tycoon, but underneath that veneer he's a very sensitive man."

"Well—" I shrugged easily "—all us girls don't get to sleep with him and find out what the real Oscar Neilsen is like."

Sudden hurt showed in her luminous blue eyes for a moment before she looked away. "Was that absolutely necessary?" she asked in a small voice.

"I was just trying out the Oscar Neilsen approach for size." I said, "but you're right, it doesn't fit too well."

Lenore looked down at her typewriter pointedly. "If you don't mind, Rick, I've got to finish this release tonight before I go home."

"I was hoping I could buy you a drink," I said.

"Thanks, but I'll have to take a rain check."

"Find out who tried to kill Carola Russo yesterday, and find out fast before they try a second time with maybe better results," I recited in a flat voice.

Lenore's head lifted sharply. "What?"

"They were my precise instructions from Oscar Neilsen." I told her. "It would be a lot easier, in one way, if I was a cop. Then I could go around asking questions like 'Where were you between the hours of noon and two P.M. on the afternoon of—?' and people would give me an answer, because I was a cop. So I could send other cops around to check the alibis I'd been given, and maybe find out who fired that gun by a process of elimination. The crime lab boys would have dug that bullet out of the workshop doorframe and I would have a report from ballistics by now. Half a dozen men would have scoured the mountain slope below the shack, and maybe found a gun, or a footprint—something."

She closed her eyes tight for a moment. "What happened back there? You suddenly lost your mind?"

"But I'm not a cop."

"So you're not a cop!" she snapped. "What do you want me to do about it? Cry a little?"

"So the best I can do is go around asking questions that people don't need to answer, or if they prefer, they can tell me lies which I can't check on," I said. "But if I get rough, needle them with a technique which is part insulting and part infuriating—maybe they'll get mad enough, or hurt enough, to blurt out some truth without thinking about it first."

"Oh!" Lenore smiled with a genuine warmth for the first time since I'd known her. "Now I understand! Just what was the truth you thought you might get from me, Rick?"

"It so happens," I admitted, "I was hoping to get some truth *into* you, honey, about Neilsen."

Her eyes were suddenly remote. "We're not about to go through all that again?"

"He uses people," I said desperately. "A lot of men do that, but Neilson uses them up, sucks them dry! It's not enough for him to just *use* other people. He has to destroy them before he'll let them go. A ride with him is a one-way ticket to the garbage dump, don't you see that?"

"Why do you hate him so much?" She looked at me almost fearfully. "You hardly know him!"

"What's that got to do with it?" I stared back at her blankly. "And who said anything about hating him?"

She turned her head away quickly. "Please go now, Rick!" Her voice was muffled and I had to strain to hear the words. "I don't want to talk about it any more, it makes me feel so—so disloyal!"

"If you don't break your relationship with Oscar Neilsen pretty goddamn soon," I said tightly, "you'll wind up in a sanitarium, Lenore! You think he'll send you flowers?"

chapter seven

There was a convertible with the top down already parked in my driveway as I came into it. I could see the back of the girl's head who was sitting in the driving seat, and had time to admire her natural dark brown hair as I got out of my own car and walked up to her.

She was still gazing steadily straight ahead of her through the windshield when I stopped beside the car door and looked down at her face.

"Well," I said softly, "as I go sex-maniac-ing on my way, taking inventory all the time! If it isn't little Janie Trent? What brings you to Holman's little grey house set slap-bang center in the heart of the status-symbol belt in Beverly Hills?"

Her pixie face was perfectly composed, the hazel eyes calmly looking straight ahead through the windshield at the fascinating vista of my closed garage door. Only a certain tightness around her mouth betrayed any tension at all.

"It was that crack last night about did it come under the heading of judicious experience for a twenty-three-year-old," she said evenly. "And that kind of fatuous grin on your stupid face as the elevator door closed!"

"How about that?" I said intelligently.

"For some crazy reason which I still don't understand," she continued in the same level voice, "I have a strong desire to explain to you exactly what I was doing at Brunhoff's apartment last night. But then, of course, there's no good reason why you should want to hear it, is there?"

"I'm always fascinated to hear the intimate details of a bachelor girl's night out in the playboy apartment," I admitted eagerly. "So come on into the house and park your fluffy little bunny-tail for a while: I'll make us a drink, and you can tell me the secrets of your lurid after-dark life on Sunset Boulevard."

"Thank you, I will!" She smiled sweetly at me as she stepped out of the car. "You sadistic, dirty-minded bum!"

A couple of minutes later she was comfortably established in an armchair at one end of my living room, a glass of Scotch in her hand, while I sat on the couch facing her, nursing a bourbon on the rocks.

Whoever the guy was who'd created the silver lamé sheath she wore with such elegance, he was not only a master of design, I realized appreciatively, but a miser with material, too. When she crossed her legs the hem automatically hiked a good four inches above her knees. Up top, the entire creation was supported by two fragile shoulder straps the width of her little finger, and the scooped neckline had the good taste to realize that even silver lamé couldn't compete with a substantial expanse of majestic cleavage, and didn't try.

"Monica Hayes is my dearest friend," Janie said in a determined voice. "I know she has her faults, but she's been kinder to me than anyone else I've ever known!"

"Kinder than she's ever been to Gallant, I wouldn't be surprised?" I said sympathetically.

An ice-cold glare from those hazel eyes had me ducking for cover in no time at all. "Okay, I'll just listen!" I promised nervously.

"The night before last I had a call from a man who said he was Sam Brunhoff," she continued in an even more determined voice. "He'd heard from a friend of a friend that I was close to Monica Hayes, and that she'd just gotten home from a location trip and found her husband missing. So I played safe and said the first part was right, anyway. Then he said Don had skipped off someplace with Carola Russo three days before and nobody knew where they were. Gino Amaldi had also gotten back into town earlier than expected, and if he found out where they were first, all hell would break loose!

"I asked him the obvious question: why was he telling me all this, instead of telling it to Monica? He just laughed and said he was naturally big-hearted, and it would sound better coming from me, her closest friend. I told him he was out of his mind if he thought I'd tell her a story like that, when I didn't even know if it was true. Up to that point he'd sounded real friendly, but then his voice changed completely, and he just snarled the whole time. 'Gallant's up in his shack in the mountains with the Italian broad,' he said. 'You don't believe me, take a run up there in the morning and find out for yourself, you dumb broad!' Then he hung up on me."

"Leaving you with the problem," I said.

Janie drank some Scotch, then shrugged her smooth bare shoulders in a quick movement, as if she wished she could shrug off her memories the same way.

"I could hardly sleep at all that night, trying to make up my mind what to do," she said in a small voice. "But in the morning I called Monica and suggested we take a run up to the cabin to take her mind off her worries, and she agreed."

She lifted her head almost defiantly and looked at me. "I thought if Brunhoff had been lying, there would be no harm done, and if he hadn't—well, maybe it was better for Monica to find out for herself, before one of her nicer friends told her the story with some added highlights of their own invention!

"When we got to the cabin, Monica saw Don's foreign sportscar parked out front and she guessed right away what was happening. She wanted me to go with her, but I said it was maybe better if she went alone because having me there the whole time would only be a further embarrassment. Well, you know the rest of the story from there."

"That takes care of yesterday afternoon," I said.

"I guess you know Neilsen called Monica from the shack?" I nodded briefly, and she continued, "I was still there when it happened, and she told me how he blackmailed her into going along with the story that Don's bullet wound had been an accident. She was terribly upset, almost hysterical about it, so I gave her a sedative and packed her off to bed. But on my way home I got to thinking about it, and it worried me. The fact remained that somebody had tried to kill Don. Supposing they tried again and succeeded? Where would that leave Monica, now that Neilsen had the others convinced it was Monica—the jealous wife—who'd tried to kill him at the shack?"

She leaned forward in the chair and looked at me earnestly. "You do see what I mean, Rick?"

"Sure," I grinned reassuringly at her. "Neilsen—or somebody using him maybe—could be setting Monica up as the fall guy for a successful attempt at murdering Gallant."

"That's it," She sighed gently, obviously relieved that I hadn't thought she was out of her mind.

"And you got to thinking about why Brunhoff had called you in the first place, and where, even before that, he'd gotten his information?" I said helpfully.

"Right!" Janie gave me a grateful smile. "I called

him at his office as soon as I got home, but he was in a playful mood! Mister-'Call me Sam, baby'-Brunhoff just wasn't having any. He kept on kidding around and wouldn't tell me a thing until finally he said if I'd give him a date that night, he'd give me the lowdown. I was so desperate then I agreed, and he told me to be at his apartment at nine-thirty last night. He'd almost forgotten—the son of a bitch roared with laughter when he said it!—his partner, Lou Martell, would be there, so bring a friend!"

Janie glared at me savagely for a moment as if I was Sam Brunhoff. "I took Sherry King with me. She's a lingerie model and knows how to look after herself: she thought it was a big deal anyway—a date with the top brass of Aria Productions!" She sneered disdainfully at the thought: "That crummy fifth-rate outfit who never made a decent movie in their lives!"

"So what happened?" I said hopefully.

"Nothing!" Her voice went flat. "I don't know what you did in there, but whatever it was you fixed it good! Brunhoff opened the door, looking like he'd just been dragged through a small sewer pipe, and told us to get the hell out again—him and his partner had work to do! Before we had a chance to say anything, he slammed the door in our faces." She smiled slowly. "I don't think poor Sherry will ever speak to me again!"

"Well, I'm now convinced that you don't belong to a call-girl syndicate specializing in giving comfort to loudmouthed film producers!" I grinned at her. "I think that calls for another drink."

I walked over to her chair and took the empty glass from her hand.

"Rick?" There was a warm glow in her hazel eyes as she looked up at me. "I wonder why it was so important to me that you wouldn't think I was just some cheap floozie, after last night?"

"Who knows?" I said easily.

"I think I'm beginning to," she said in a soft voice. When I returned with the fresh drinks, Janie had moved from the armchair to the couch, and patted the vacant space beside her for me to sit there. Once I did, she turned toward me, resting one arm on the back of the couch while she looked intently into my face, and I was conscious of her knee thrusting hard against mine.

"Well," she said huskily, "tell me the story of your life, Rick Holman!"

"That's a sordid story," I said. "You wouldn't want to hear it."

She leaned closer toward me, so that one casual glance sent me glassy-eyed at the staggering amount of cleavage revealed by the gaping neckline.

"Then tell me why, after I've gone to all this trouble to prove to you I'm not a floozie," she murmured softly, "I'm acting like one right now?"

"It would be nice to think you're about to make one of these decisions in favor of a new judicious experience," I told her. "But I'm too humble a character to hope for that!"

She laughed, and it sounded like a purring tigress, then pulled me toward her. Her lips were cool against mine for a moment, then she pulled her head away and placed the flat of her hands against my chest. A moment later her lips returned, while her hands explored my chest and spine in small caressing movements that were calculated to send me into a wild frenzy any time now.

It was the kind of a game that needed two players, I figured—double your pleasure, double your fun!—so I placed both hands, but not flat, on her chest, and was about to explore all that wonderful territory in a similar small series of caressing movements, when she pulled right away from me to the far end of the couch.

"Not right now, Rick!" She hastily tugged the finger-straps back onto her shoulders. "It's—it's too sudden!" The smile of apology was strictly an afterthought, I noted.

"Whatever you say, Janie," I told her humbly.

She picked up her glass and drank some Scotch like she needed it, then smiled again. "You're a lousy conversationalist, Rick Holman! Tell me a story, a story about your work—if you won't talk about yourself?" Her knee slid forward again and touched mine, with a kind of tentative pressure that promised a reward when the story was told.

"Because I resent that crack about me being a lousy conversationalist, Janie honey," I said cheerfully, "I'll tell you the most fascinating story you've heard in a long time. It's not only fascinating—it's the funniest story you ever heard. You'll die laughing, I promise! And, the way all great stories should be, it's about someone you know very well!"

Her eyes searched my face quickly for a clue, then she licked her lips and smiled cautiously. "It sounds like fun, Rick! Go right ahead."

"I visited with Don Gallant this afternoon," I said, for a beginning. "That guy may be very big at the box office, but he's still a creep for me! You know the only way he can make any conversation is to scrape up lines of dialogue from his old movies?"

"Well," she said, shrugging, "everybody has their own opinion about Don—but go on!"

"I met his nurse on the way upstairs," I continued, "and she was the sexiest nurse I've ever seen! A blonde with an incredible balcony, and the way she wiggled when—"

"You can skip the anatomical detail!" she grated.

"Oh, okay!" I gave her a hurt look, but she chose to let it go right on by. "Well, when I got into the bedroom, there he was watching television. . . ."

I plowed through the whole story, leaving nothing out, giving my relentless attention to the smallest detail. After what seemed like a hell of a long time, I finally reached the climax.

"Can't you just imagine it?" I gurgled with laughter. "There's Don—frantic to prove to her there's nothing wrong with his virility—maybe talking nice and making an occasional halfhearted pass at her, when suddenly she tells him to stop bleeding, because she's been crazy for him all the time. Then she whips off her white uniform, pulls back the covers and—with her magnificent bosom heaving with passion—leaps right in beside him!"

I held my sides as I howled with laughter. "Isn't that a riot?"

"I think that's about the dirtiest, most despicable trick I've ever heard!" a granite-like voice said. "It must take a very special type of stinkingly perverted mind to think up something as low and disgusting as that!"

I stopped laughing suddenly when I saw Janie's white face set in a frozen mask of fury, and the cold venomous glitter in her eyes.

"Why, honey!" I said, like I was amazed. "I thought you'd love that story knowing yourself just what kind of a slob Don Gallant is?" I gulped, and tried again. "I mean, you being Monica's best friend, and all?"

"You filth!" she whispered.

"You bitch!" I said right back.

"What?" She quivered, as if I'd hit her across the face.

"Monica's best friend!" I sneered. "With you as her best friend, Janie, she doesn't need enemies, right?"

"Are you insane?" she whispered harshly.

"Maybe you started out as Monica's best friend, but once you met her husband everything was different?" I leaned against the back of the couch, and lit a cigarette. "From then on you were both Monica's best friend and and Don's favorite lover—and because it was going on right under her nose, Monica never even noticed, I bet?"

She tried to meet my eyes and couldn't. "That's utterly fantastic!" The words had a hollow, leaden sound to them.

"That's why—after Brunhoff called and told you about Don being up at the shack with Carola Russo— you couldn't wait to get Monica up there and find out if it was true. Being the kind of dame you are, honey, you'd soon swallow your own gall and start seeing the possible advantages of the situation. Maybe Monica would be so mad about it, she'd divorce him, even? You'd be damned sure in your own mind, that once you had a chance to sink your claws into Gallant legally, he'd never have the chance to be free of them again!"

"This is some weird fantasy right out of your own head," she insisted, with the dull sound of defeat in her voice.

"You sure didn't look worried about your best friend when I arrived up there," I grated. "You even went out of your way to delay me going inside for as long as you could, with a whole spiel of terribly bright, seductive conversation—remember? The more time Monica had inside the cabin with Gallant, the madder she'd get at him, you figured. Only the whole thing turned out to be a bust, because he wasn't there at all.

"For sure, you worked on her outraged feelings all the way home in the car." I continued savagely, "knowing that if Monica did give the papers the whole story, her pride—and her own public image—would force her to go for a divorce. But then that was a bust, too, when Neilsen blackmailed her into keeping quiet. The shooting worried you a little, and not knowing who it was that told Brunhoff you were Don's lover, worried you even more. If whoever it was could tell Brunhoff about you, there was nothing to stop them telling other people—like Monica, for example?

"I think you told the truth for once, about calling Brunhoff and asking him for the name of his informant. But when he played hard to get, I'll bet it was your very own idea to suggest a passionate evening in his apartment, in return for the name you wanted so badly!"

I suddenly laughed again. "And even *that* turned out to be a bust! I'd been there before you and left Brunhoff in a strictly unreceptive mood. So the only thing left for you to do was what you did tonight. Dream up some excuse for visiting with me, and find out what I knew, and what Brunhoff had told me last night." I shook my head slowly. "Incidentally, that 'tease now, pay later' technique is pretty corny! You must lose out more times than you win that way—"

"Aren't you through yet?" Janie said wearily. "You sound like your needle's stuck!"

"Sure, I'm all through," I agreed. "You want to kiss me again before you leave?"

"You creep!" She shuddered in revulsion at the very thought.

"I know who it was that told Brunhoff about you and Don Gallant, baby!" I lied, with a knowing leer on my face.

She just sat there staring at me for a while, and I realized I'd never really known before just what a conflict of emotions was, until that moment. It was kind of exciting for a while—wondering if just one face could stand up to all that torture without splintering into small fragments. But good old Janie came through in the end! Fear, greed, and avarice won out again!

Janie got up from the couch listlessly and just stood there for a few seconds, with her eyes closed and the palms of her hands pressed tight against her cheeks. Then she slowly opened her eyes again and gave me a passable imitation of a smile.

"All right, Rick," she said softly, "you won."

She pushed the fingerstraps off her shoulders, then tucked one arm behind her back and gave the zip-fastener a sharp tug.

"Hold it!" I yelped, but it was too late.

The silver lamé dress glittered at her feet, and she stepped out of it daintily, wearing a pair of white nylon briefs. I was struck numb without warning; vaguely my mind guessed that any girl lucky enough to be endowed with that kind of natural uplift wouldn't dream of wearing a bra, and that was why she didn't. It also occurred to me it was getting a little late to tell her I didn't really have the name she wanted so badly, anyway.

Janie shook her head from side to side and her dark

brown hair tumbled around her face in wanton disarray. Then she arched her back slightly and ran her hands down over the curve of her hips, so they made a silken whispering sound. Then, these rites completed, she moved toward me in a sensual, undulating kind of glide that was guaranteed to send an octogenarian clean out of his mind.

"Hold it!" I whimpered. "Janie! I was putting you on—I never got the name from Brunhoff!"

"What?" There was a slurred quality to her voice, as if she was talking in her sleep.

"You're wasting your time, honey!" I yelped. "I don't know the name!"

"*What!*" She came to an abrupt stop and her whole body went rigid.

"I'm sorry," I apologized, "it was a lousy thing to do. It's just that I get mad when somebody calls me a creep! I didn't mean to let you get this far, I only wanted to prove a point."

"You're just like the rest of all the smug, virtuous little men, aren't you?" she said bitterly. "You get that way trying to keep your naturally lecherous instincts bottled up inside! Only there are times when you see your chance to get the best of both worlds, like now?"

"Janie, you're right," I said humbly. "I *am* a creep!"

"Who cares?" She flopped onto the couch beside me and groaned horribly.

"What's the matter?" I gurgled.

"Rick Holman, be honest with me!" She brushed a long strand of dark brown hair away from her face and looked hard at me, the corners of her mouth trembling a little. "Would you say this is one of my off-days?"

Before I could answer, she threw herself against my chest and buried her head in my shoulder. I patted her back in a vaguely consoling manner, while her shoulders heaved convulsively and the firm weight of her breasts gently bounced against my chest. Right then I experienced my own conflict of emotions, and it wasn't easy.

Janie lifted her head after a while, and it was only

then that I realized the tears streaming down her face were tears of laughter.

"What's funny?" I gaped at her.

"Me—you—everything!" she gurgled. "You don't realize how desperate I am to know who tipped off Brunhoff about me! But that was my last desperate throw! There I was, stripped right down to my panties, working like a mad thing at being exotic and erotic at the same time—and you casually mention you don't know the name, anyway!" Another spasm of laughter shook her body. "If there's anything more a girl can do after that, all I can say is, nobody ever told me!"

"I'm sorry," I said again. "It was my fault—"

"Rick?" She slid one hand inside my shirt and dug her nails cruelly into my tender flesh until I yelped. "Promise me one thing? That you won't be so damned smug in future, even when you are right?"

"If you promise me that in future you'll see a creep like Don Gallant for what he really is," I said.

"I promise!" she said solemnly. "Don Gallant is a creep!"

"I promise!" I echoed her solemn tones. "I promise not to be a smug bastard ever again! A bastard, maybe —but smug?—never!"

"Good!" she said contentedly, and leaned against my chest again.

"What do we do now?" I muttered.

"I'd feel kind of stupid if I took off that dress for nothing," she said thoughtfully. "Why don't we make love, Rick?" She turned her head a fraction and nibbled my earlobe for a few moments. "Somehow this has turned into a genuine judicious experience for me!"

"Me, too, honey," I said quickly. "Me, too!"

Maybe five minutes later she suddenly laughed again, and my mind was about to become unhinged because it was so much the wrong time and the wrong place for it.

"That was funny?" I muttered hoarsely.

"I'm sorry, lover." It sounded like genuine remorse in Janie's voice. "I just remembered about Don, and that eager-beaver nurse! You think she could have loved him to death by now?"

"Who knows?" I grinned, in spite of all the things working against my sense of humor right then. "At this very moment she could be preparing Gallant for a small featured role in her next production!"

Janie gave a wild shriek and rolled right off the couch. It was one hell of a way to make love!

chapter eight

The phone rang at about ten of nine the next morning while Janie was in the shower. I answered it and Oscar Neilsen's rich deep bass said he wanted to see me in his office right away, I was to hotfoot it over there, and if he'd only known what a completely useless son of a bitch I was in the first place, he never would have hired me. All this, so perfectly articulated, so early in the morning, I thought bleakly as I hung up.

Janie came out of the bathroom a couple of minutes later, wearing my favorite silk shirt which just reached the tops of her thighs. "Breakfast in five minutes, lover," she said, and kept on going toward the kitchen.

"Not for me," I snarled, and told her about Neilsen's call.

"That's too bad, lover," she said sympathetically. "I don't know that I'll have any, either. The best hands in the business have a ten-thirty appointment with a commercial, and I don't think they'd approve of me wearing that little lamé number while I plunge up to the elbows in foaming detergent?"

"We all have our problems," I said gloomily. "When do I see you again?"

"I think the smart thing for me to do is write off last night to the mad folly of the moment," she said easily. "You're a dead loss to me career-wise, Holman! Since when could you get me into the movies?"

"And I thought you were a reformed character after last night?" I said in an injured voice.

"You're one hell of a reformer, kid!" She winked at me, and left me stunned at the ribald implications she packed into just one twitch of an eyelid. "Why don't you call me when your resistance is running low?" she suggested.

"That would be a great idea except for one thing," I growled. "I don't have your number."

"I'll write it down for you and leave it by the phone," she said placidly. "You'd better get going. Goodby, lover, and don't get smug again before the next time."

"Say it once more before I go," I said sternly.

"Don Gallant is a creep!" she recited submissively.

I took one last look at her as I opened the door; her back was toward me as she moved toward the kitchen, snapping her fingers in the air to the rhythm of her own pagan version of the cha-cha. I wistfully figured that silk shirt of mine never had it so good, then resolutely turned my face toward the harsh world of reality that waited for me on the front porch.

Lenore Palmer's office had impressed me the first time I saw it, but Oscar Neilsen's left me stunned when I walked into it a few minutes later. It took me a couple of seconds to refocus my eyes, and adjust to the fact that those foreshortened lonely-looking objects, half-buried in an acre of overgrown wall to wall carpet at the far end of the room, were actually a desk, and a chair, with Neilsen himself sitting in it.

The native gunbearer—who looked almost like a personal secretary—had disappeared back into the outer office, leaving me to make the safari alone. A visitor's chair popped out of the carpet about six feet this side of his desk, and I sank into it gratefully.

Neilsen looked at me for a few seconds with his usual saintlike expression, then consulted his strap watch carefully.

"What took you so long?" he said.

I gave him a cold stare. "The wind was against me," I said.

"Don't give me any of your cute repartee," he said coldly. "I don't have time for it. Do you realize it's getting close to forty-eight hours since I hired you, Holman, and thus far I haven't heard even one goddam word from you!"

"I liked you better when you called me by my first name," I said. "Not much, but better."

His fingers drummed a soft tattoo on the desktop for a few moments, then he deliberately relaxed and pushed himself deeper into his chair. "All right," he said softly, "so I am a little on edge this morning! But I have a six-million-dollar commitment swinging in the balance here. If anything happens to Carola Russo, the whole package flies over the transom, Rick. You'll admit to my having some rights to an early-morning temper, surely?"

"I guess so," I said, nodding generously. "What do you want from me?—a progress report?"

"Anything I can get," he said, and sighed. "Are you making any progress at all?"

"You remember that bit about you not believing in coincidence? Did you find out for sure if Amaldi was tipped off in Rome, about what was happening here with Carola and Gallant?" I queried.

"He got an unsigned cable to that effect," Neilsen said. "Showed it to me yesterday."

"Monica Hayes was tipped off in a more subtle kind of way," I told him. "Her best friend, Janie Trent, got a call from Sam Brunhoff laying it on the line. Sam suggested if she didn't believe him, why didn't she talk Monica into taking a drive up to the mountains and finding out for herself."

"The hell you say! Sam Brunhoff?" There was a momentary gleam in the mild blue eyes. "Just how did Sam come by all his facts?"

"It's a good question, but not a vital one," I said. "I talked to Sam, and Lou Martell, the night before last. They denied any part of the shooting, naturally, then got indignant about the way you double-crossed them with those personal, not company, contracts you signed with all the people important to the production. They seemed especially sore about the fifty thousand for Gallant's agent you took them for, and what really hurt, apparently, was the way you repaid it with stock in Aria Productions."

A beatific smile lit up his whole face for a moment. "I have to admit I was secretly rather pleased with that one, myself! What else?"

"The way they tell it, you're everything you say they are!"

"But you haven't heard my side of the story yet, Rick," he said pleasantly.

"I have indeed!" I grunted. "Lenore Palmer gave it to me late yesterday afternoon, complete with flashing eyes and heaving bosom. I hadn't realized you were the Albert Schweitzer of the film industry before, but she made it all very clear!"

"So much loyalty from one of my executives makes me feel truly humble, Rick." His face selected a suitable expression for the occasion and put it on. "Tell me—I ask only out of idle curiosity—where was Lenore when she declaimed so nobly in my defense? In her office? —or your bed?"

"You know damned well she lives in your bed, figuratively speaking," I said grinning. "I had a long session with Carola at your house yesterday morning, and all I know is she's convinced the last person in the world who wants her dead is Poppa Gino."

"Which only proves her emotional involvement with Gino Amaldi," Neilsen sneered.

"Right," I agreed with him.

"What else?"

"Nothing!"

"Nothing?" His mouth tightened a little. "You must be joking, Rick? I hire the top man in his field—entirely on his own terms!—and after forty-eight hours, this is all you can tell me?"

"I told you at the beginning," I snapped, "that it wasn't easy and it could take a long time. I was wrong about that—it will take forever! You were right, I'm convinced of it, that those shots were fired at Carola Russo, and Gallant was unlucky enough to get in the way of the first one. But there's no chance of ever finding out who fired the gun now. Maybe there was just a slim chance in the beginning if the police had been brought into it right after it happened, but you couldn't afford to do that. So now all you have left is a choice between two possibilities.

"The first is that Amaldi organized it in a fit of jealousy and he may do it again—or it's quite probable he's calmed down now and almost forgotten it ever happened. The second is that your ex-partner and his buddy organized it, as a payoff for the way you double-crossed them in the first place. If Brunhoff and Martell are in back of it, you'll never prove it and you've got no chance of stopping them from killing the girl in a second attempt."

"Is that all?" Neilsen murmured.

"The only advice I can offer is kind of stinking, and I know it!" I said coldly. "But the only way to ensure the girl's life is by keeping a close watch on Amaldi the whole time—*and* making some kind of a deal with Brunhoff and Martell."

He sat in silence for quite a long time, then his fingers drummed the desktop slowly so it sounded like a death march.

"There is nothing else you can do?" he asked.

"Where's Amaldi now?"

"At my house."

"I might go out there and take a last crack at him," I said with no enthusiasm in my voice. "I doubt if it will get us anyplace but it's worth a try."

"I agree you should try," he said flatly. "If you fail, as you obviously expect to, what then?"

"That's it!"

"I'm left with your educated advice?" He laughed, mostly to himself. "Watch Amaldi night and day in case he tries again—and go crawling back on my belly to Sam Brunhoff and Lou Martell pleading for a deal? I love your advice, Rick!"

"I said it was kind of stinking," I reminded him.

"Tell me one more thing before you disappear from my life completely?" His voice was suddenly full of high good humor. "Do you expect to get paid for your educated advice?"

"You mean you won't pay me for it?" I rasped.

"Rick!" His beautiful bass voice chided me gently, for even having the doubt. "I always meet my bills! I'm perfectly willing to pay for your advice on the basis of its worth. To me it's worth—a nickel?" He held up his hand as if I'd made a violent protest. "All right, Rick. Bill me for a dime and I probably won't argue!"

He leaned back in his chair comfortably and watched me, with something that looked like a good-natured smile on his face. I met his gaze easily, and put something that looked like a pleasant smile onto my own face—and suddenly it was a test of endurance. We sat smiling grimly at each other for a minor eternity, and I was glad it was Neilsen who broke first.

"No protest?" There was an underlying rasp to his bantering tone. "Then you agree, Rick, that my price is fair and just?"

"Don't knock yourself out trying," I said easily. "You'll never make it, friend."

He frowned for a moment. "Could you rephrase that, Rick, so I can understand what it is you're trying to convey? You are trying to tell me something?"

"You'll never sink your hooks into me, Oscar, because I won't let you do it," I told him. "You survive by destroying other people—thrive, in fact, on their destruction. Once you can get an emotional response from anybody, you've got him hooked. Then you sink your hooks in deeper and deeper the whole time until that person is completely destroyed and you have to go look for a new victim. You're an expert at arousing emotional responses, because they're your tools of trade, like love, fear and hate. Hate maybe is your speciality, wouldn't you say, Oscar?"

His hands gripped the edge of his desk as he stared at me; then the suntanned, unwrinkled face slowly set into a mask of cold, implacable fury, and the saintlike image was destroyed forever.

"But I arouse no emotional response in you, Rick?" His voice crackled with suppressed rage.

"None at all," I assured him. I got up from the chair and stood in front of the desk looking down at him for a moment.

"To me," I explained in a clear voice, "you are a parasite on the face of humanity, Oscar. Who ever heard of a human being getting emotionally involved with a parasite?"

I started back across the acre of carpet, thinking happily that, even if the whole assignment had been unprofitable, I'd just gotten good value from the nickel, anyway.

The morning sun shone down with equal brilliance on Neilsen's house in the Palisades, and the rest of Greater Los Angeles, demonstrating its impartiality once again. I parked the car on the raked driveway in front of the house, then walked up onto the porch and rang the doorbell.

A tall, lean, sinewy-looking character opened the front door and stared at me impassively. His thick black hair was neatly slicked down across his head, and the pomade was still too highly scented for my taste. I had a momentary weird feeling that somebody had made a movie the previous morning with me and the star, and now they were running it through again.

"This is getting to be a habit, Mr. Holman," the sinewy-looking character said in a flat voice.

"Hello there, Tino." I smiled vaguely at him. "That houseman bit was cute."

"I figured it might worry you a little." His dark eyes sneered at me. "You look like a worrier, Mr. Holman!"

"I haven't stopped worrying about you from the time I left here yesterday, Tino." I murmured. "I hardly slept at all last night, worrying if I'd hurt your feelings out by the pool."

"That crack about me spoiling the view?" He shook his head slightly. "It didn't worry me, Mr. Holman. Well, maybe it did at the time, but later on I realized you must have been under a great mental strain, and it didn't worry me any more."

"A great mental strain?" I queried.

"Making up your mind to take Miss Russo by brute force," he said blandly. "I watched the two of you rolling around in the grass through my binoculars, and it was better than television. Sorry you lost, Mr. Holman!" He smiled thinly. "For a moment there, it was like we had the mad dogs running loose all over the grounds again!"

"I'm expected, of course?" I said. "All this swinging dialogue couldn't be impromptu—you've been practicing before I got here?"

"Mr. Amaldi is out by the pool with Miss Russo." He made a formal announcement out of it.

"Thank you." I lit a cigarette, without hurrying the small ritual at all. "You know something, Tino? I never talked with a big executive's personal assistant before, and I find it's fascinating, in a macabre kind of way. What does a personal assistant do before he is one? I mean, how do you start out on that kind of career?"

"By minding your own business, mostly!" he grunted.

"That's not what I heard," I said firmly. "The best way to start is running errands for some big man who's got real talent spread over a wide field of diverse activities—somebody like Lou Martell, for example?"

"Like you said, Mr. Holman," he said, smiling wearily. "Mr. Martell is a big man with a real talent!"

"I guess you see him often?" I said idly. "Talk over old times, and all?"

"No, I don't!" he snapped.

"You must have been a valuable man to Lou, Tino?" I protested. "I bet you did all the nasty jobs for him— the real messy ones that you have to do just right or you never get a second chance at them, well, not under twenty years, anyway!" I smiled warmly. "Lou couldn't forget anybody who'd taken care of the rough ones for him—he's just not that kind of guy. When was the last time you got together with Lou and had a gabfest over old times?—and the new times, too?"

"I've never seen Lou—not once!—from the time I went to Europe with Mr. Neilsen!" His voice shook for a moment. "I got an idea what you're trying to do to me, Holman, but it won't work, understand?"

"So maybe you talk on the phone a little?" I beamed at him. "What's to worry about?"

"Just don't try it, Holman," he said thickly, "that's all!"

"Take it easy, Tino," I said. "I wouldn't want you to run out of steam halfway through the morning."

"You got a real friend now, Holman, you know that, don't you?" he whispered. "I'm going to be looking out for you all the time!" Then he gently closed the door in my face.

I walked around the house to the back, and spotted the two figures beside the pool. When I got real close, I saw Carola was lying facedown this time, the top of her red cotton bikini undone and held firmly by the weight of her breasts, so the ties wouldn't get in the way while Gino Amaldi rubbed the oil into her back. There was something almost pagan about the flawless lines of her body; the inverted arrowhead from her shoulders down to her tiny waist—the high curve of her taut rump—the poetry of long, slender legs.

Amaldi made a grotesque contrast as he squatted beside her like some bald-headed satyr. The sweat rolled down his sloping chest and flabby paunch unceasingly, and the massive arms and legs, covered with thick black hair, looked too big for the stunted body. His bright red shorts covered with white polka dots didn't exactly improve the overall picture, either.

He lifted his head slowly and looked at me, his soiled-looking brown eyes devoid of any expression. Then he grunted.

"You look like you're working hard this morning," I said politely.

I saw Carola's body stiffen at the sound of my voice.

"That's enough, Poppa Gino," she said. "Do me up!"

His short stubby fingers fumbled with the ties until he finally had them tied in a clumsy bow. Carola rolled over onto her back, then came up into a sitting position. The bow Amaldi had tied must have been loose, because the bikini top slipped down suddenly, revealing the full grandeur of her breasts as she sat up. For a moment I gazed numbly at the startling contrast between their coral-peaked alabaster whiteness and the deep brown tan that covered the rest of her body.

Then Carola readjusted the red cotton strip with no sign of embarrassment, and reached casually behind her back with both hands to tie the bow tighter. Liquid-sounding Italian bubbled from her lips, and when Amaldi answered her with a ferocious scowl, she threw back her head and laughed gleefully. A few moments later she looked directly at me for the first time, and the laughter died abruptly in her throat.

"How is the jungle today, Carola?" I said softly.

The jade-green eyes glittered with some indefinable quality as she stared silently into my face. I felt the hot sun on my face, and sensed the absolute concentration of the gorilla-like Amaldi as he squatted on his haunches, watching the two of us. High in a treetop a bird screeched suddenly, then zoomed up into the sky.

"I said, leave me alone!" she whispered. "Why won't you do as I ask? What have I ever done to you!"

"He got an anonymous cable while he was in Rome, which told him about you and Gallant," I said slowly. "Did he tell you about it?"

"It doesn't matter!" she said bitterly. "If I could only find some way to make you understand that!"

"It gave him lots of time to think." I said, ignoring her outburst. "Sitting high above the clouds he wouldn't be able to think of anything else. And it would be getting bigger—in his mind—all the time. A man of strong primitive passions, Gino Amaldi! A man capable of nursing an emotion like simple jealousy until it grew into something much bigger, like hate, maybe?"

"I do not understand all the words," Amaldi said irritably.

"He says you are a jealous man, Poppa Gino," Carola told him in an expressionless voice, without moving her eyes from my face. "He says you got a cable in Rome which told you about me and the actor."

"It is finished, *cara.*" His tone of voice dismissed the whole thing completely. "I beat you, and you are sorry you did a stupid thing. So, it is finished!"

"You hear that, Rick Holman?" she said in a tight voice. "It's all over? He beat me, and I was sorry for what I did?"

"You used him, and he used you?" I sneered gently, "That mutual arrangement's working just fine again, isn't it?"

"Just fine!" she snapped.

"Again!" Amaldi groaned. "I do not understand, *cara?*"

"It was nothing important, Poppa Gino." She smiled mockingly at me. "Nothing at all."

"He will go soon?" he asked hopefully. "I don't like him so close all the time." His voice became indignant. "Last time we meet, he knock me down for no reason at all! He's a crazy man!"

"You're so right, Poppa Gino!" Carola laughed happily. "You hear that, Rick Holman? You're a crazy man. So go away and leave us alone, crazy man, because we don't like you being so close all the time!"

"I'll go," I said. "This was the last time—that one more try for lonely, lost little Carola Russo! I should have stayed home. Like the man says, you were a nothing when he discovered you, and he's been smart enough to keep you exactly the same way, and now you've gotten so used to the idea, it feels good. It may be a kind of lousy ambition—to want to be a nothing—but I'll say this for you, honey, you sure made it!"

She turned her head away in an abrupt gesture. "Leave me *alone?*"

"For always," I promised.

"You go now?" Amaldi asked hopefully.

"Yes," I nodded and smiled politely. "I go now, you predatory, prehensile, primeval monstrosity!" I spoke in a real friendly, warm-sounding voice, still smiling at him the whole time. "I sincerely hope the day will soon come when your anthropoid antics and simian similarities will induce some curator of a zoological institution to incarcerate your carcass within its encaged confines!"

He beamed up at me, nodding his head vigorously the whole time. "Is good?"

"Is great!" I snarled, then turned and walked back toward the house.

Tino was waiting for me when I got back to the car, with his back resting against the hood. His dark eyes searched my face for a moment, then he smiled slyly.

"I guess it makes you stop and think for a moment, huh, Mr. Holman?"

"What?" I grunted.

"When a dish like her prefers an ape like him, to a— you name it!—like yourself?"

"I don't have to do anything about you." I told him,

as I slid behind the wheel. "After a while you'll grow warts all over your face!"

"That's way below your usual style, Mr. Holman," he said sorrowfully. "I guess you took a real beating from the Italian broad, huh?"

"Goodbye, Tino!" I bared my teeth at him, then started the motor. "Get yourself a big green toad for when the warts come, because they rub off against a toadskin—either that, or it gives the toad warts. You experiment when the times comes?"

I shifted into drive and the car leaped forward, the rear wheels busy converting the raked drive into an unraked drive.

"Hold it!" Tino shouted frantically.

"What?" I stopped the car for a moment, as he ran to catch up.

"There was a call for you," he panted. "Mr. Neilsen said for you to go straight to the office and see Miss Palmer, and it's real urgent!"

"Cheez!" I looked at him savagely. "How about that? You figure if I get there real quick, maybe he'll give me the chance to make another nickel?"

chapter nine

The public relations director was on her lunch hour, I figured, because she had a sandwich in one hand and the phone in the other when I walked into her office. She smiled brightly and waved the sandwich toward the eggshell-shaped chair, and suddenly it was like old times before Oscar Neilsen had devalued my services.

Lenore finished her phone call and hung up, took a savage bite of her sandwich, then smiled again and mumbled indistinctly, "Hi, Rick!"

"Hi, Lenore," I said. "I'm waiting to hear from you, but I don't mind sitting and waiting until you get back from that sandwich. I'll find something to keep me amused—maybe I'll grow a beard, who knows?"

She swallowed convulsively, then looked at me with a pained expression on her face. "You're nothing but a brute! And I only eat that way because I'm hungry."

"On you, it looks good," I conceded. "What is the urgent news from the desk of Oscar Neilsen?"

"I have it right here." Her fingers scrabbled frantically through the pile of papers on her desk, then stopped suddenly. "Here it is!" She studied it for a moment, then shrugged. "Well, if it makes any sense to you?"

"Read it to me?" I suggested.

" 'Tell Holman I have decided to take his advice,' " Lenore read slowly. " 'Therefore its value has increased significantly' (that's underlined three or four times) 'and I have arranged meeting with Brunhoff and Martell at my house tonight, nine-thirty, to discuss deal. Imperative Holman be there as precautionary measure —do not take no for an answer—his fee is guaranteed!' "

Lenore dropped the paper back onto the desk. "That's it! Does it make any sense to you?"

"I guess so," I said grudgingly. "Thanks, Lenore."

"I wish I could do more!" She bowed her head gracefully. "What's new, Rick?"

"I have a hot flash for you," I murmured in a confidential voice. "The big secret romance between Janie Trent and Don Gallant has permanently lapsed into the off-again file!"

"I'm not surprised!" Lenore sniffed contemptuously. "It can't be more than two weeks back, when he confided his big new romance was that girl Janie Trent, and this was *it!*"

"And had to be kept a big secret because she happened to be his wife's best friend!" I chuckled.

"But, of course!" Lenore gave me a cynical grin. "Or it just might spoil a beautiful friendship!"

"Sure," I said vaguely. "There's something else while I think of it. I owe you an apology for last night."

"Don't worry about it, Rick!" Her luminous blue eyes were friendly. "You were trying to give me good advice, as you saw it."

"I hadn't realized then you'd already given yourself the same advice—and taken it!" I added.

She patted her short-cut blond hair with one hand, while she looked at me blankly. "I don't get it."

"What I said last night was basically that Neilsen

destroys people; he was destroying you, and you should fight back," I said easily. "I didn't know you already had fought back. My congratulations!"

"I'm sorry, Rick—" she smiled uncertainly "—but I still don't understand."

"I had Tino figured for the inside leak," I explained. "But on the way into town I thought he'd have gone to Martell, not Brunhoff. Tipping off Amaldi was no problem, because it only meant sending him an unsigned cable; but giving the good word to Monica Hayes was a problem, I guess?"

"Rick?" Her voice almost had a ring of conviction. "Are you out of your mind?"

"But you'd worked for Sam Brunhoff long before Neilsen broke away and set up his own company," I said. "I'll bet he was tickled pink when you told him about Gallant and the Russo girl keeping house up in the mountains—then explained the sure way to spring an avenging Monica Hayes on them was to tell Janie Trent all about it, because Janie wasn't only Monica's best friend, she was also Don Gallant's brand new secret romance. It was a real cute idea, Lenore, and it protected you very effectively. Sam Brunhoff wouldn't throw away his chances of further invaluable inside information by exposing you, of course.

"I wondered before why you didn't call me the same afternoon Neilsen told you to, and left it until the next morning." I smiled at her. "You didn't want me to get there before Monica, of course?"

The beautiful oval face was a sickly gray color, as she stared at me like a hypnotized rabbit. "I'm sorry," she whispered, "I don't know what you're talking about!"

"Come on, Lenore!" I said impatiently. "I'm not about to tell Neilsen! You little secret's safe with me."

"He knows!" A look of despair showed in her eyes. "I'm sure of it, but somehow he doesn't care about what I did. But he knows, and he's making sure I appreciate the fact. Remember when he bawled me

out in the cabin? 'You're not getting any younger,' he said. And then that charming thought about an old maid's traumas and sexual fantasies?"

"I remember," I said truthfully.

"I've been his mistress since that first year in Europe," she said, with a kind of wistful pride in her voice. "When we came back, we moved into that house in the Palisades together. That afternoon, after I'd taken Gallant home in the ambulance, I came back here to pick up a couple of things. Everything I own was stacked in an untidy heap in back of my desk; clothes, jewelry, suitcases, books—everything! There was a note on the desk which said the locks of the house had been changed, and if I ever dared mention one word of this to him at any time, I would be out of a job as well as his bed!"

"The cruelty I dig," I said slowly, "but killing a relationship that had lasted three years or more, in one shot like that, was kind of abrupt, even for an Oscar Neilsen, wasn't it?"

Lenore's wide mouth set in a bitter curve. "I knew it was coming! From that first time he met Gino Amaldi and Carola Russo. I watched his face when he talked to the Italian girl, and I knew! Throwing me out of his life was just housecleaning from Oscar's point of view. He was getting ready for the new tenant, but I don't think she'll ever arrive!"

"Because of Amaldi?" I said.

"Maybe," Lenore said tightly, "but most of all, the girl herself. She can't stand the sight of Oscar Neilsen! It even shows in her eyes when he walks into the same room she's in. I think she'd kill herself, if he was the only alternative." Her luminous eyes shone with a wistful hope. "Or maybe she might even kill him first?"

I wore a thirty-eight in a belt holster that night, because I figured the only reason Neilsen wanted me out there while he talked about a deal with his former partners, was to act as additional protection for Carola

Russo, just in case Brunhoff and Martell tried to start anything.

The whole house was a blaze of light when I got there a couple of minutes after nine; even the pool was floodlit, like it was going to be a big party. Or maybe Neilsen was feeling a little nervous, and figured the lights would stop anybody sneaking up close. The actual effect they had was to provide a perimeter of well-lighted ground, extending about twenty feet out from the house, all around. Then, directly beyond that was an impenetrable darkness, where a whole goddamn army could hide, knowing it would be impossible to be seen from inside the house.

Tino, as always, opened the front door to me and said I was early, in a tone of voice that vaguely implied there was no chance they'd waited dinner, anyway.

"Where is everybody?" I asked him.

"Out on the back terrace." He gestured vaguely toward the interior of the house. "Through there, and all the silver's counted!"

"I'll concentrate on jewelry and the wall safe, then," I promised. "That is, if you've left anything worthwhile?"

"I just can't wait to see you making all those real funny remarks when Lou Martell gets here!" His dark eyes leered at me. "Lou is a guy with a real short temper, Holman, and my guess is he'll cut you down to size so fast, you won't even know what's happened until your chin hits the floor!"

"I thought he was coming here to talk with Neilsen?" I said mildly. "But I won't argue if you tell me he's coming to talk with me, Tino, because you're the boy with the direct wire to Lou, so you can chat over old times whenever you have the inclination, right?"

"You start saying things like that where Neilsen can hear you," he hissed, "and I'll cut your heart out!"

"Suddenly you seem to have lost that delightfully brittle sense of humor you once had, Tino," I said regretfully. "Why don't you go look for it, while I'm looking for the route to the back exit?"

Apart from a couple of detours, I managed to find my way through the house without any real trouble, and emerged onto the back terrace in one piece. Oscar Neilsen detached himself from the small group standing at the edge of the terrace admiring the floodlit pool, and came across to where I stood.

"You're early, Rick!"

"I know," I grunted. "Tino told me when he opened the front door."

"It's a good thing, we can talk before Brunhoff and Martell get here," he said. "You know why I wanted you here tonight?"

"Added protection for Carola, just in case they try something?" I suggested.

"That's about it," he said, nodding. "I want Tino inside the house the whole time while I'm in conference with the other two. Otherwise Lou might sneak five or six of his men inside, while I'm still happily talking percentages! Tino knows the house backwards, and he also knows most of the tricks Lou might be tempted to try on for size.

"So you're here for just one thing, Rick! Guard Carola the whole time, and never let her out of your sight. I've already told the others that's what you're here for, and suggested you all stay right here on the terrace until the meeting's finished. I guess that's about all."

"What made you change your mind and take my advice?" I asked interestedly.

"The repulsive logic behind it!" He chuckled softly. "I did mention in that note I left with Lenore, that the price has gone up?"

"You did," I agreed. "Do I have a whole quartet yet?"

"I think you'll be completely satisfied, Rick, when this whole thing is wound up, and you see my check," he said easily. "Why don't we join the others?" He checked his watch. "It's only a quarter after nine, now. They won't be early, because they'll think it might make them look overanxious!"

"And are they?" I queried.

"When I called Sam and suggested this meeting to discuss a deal, I could hear him panting at the other end!" Neilsen chuckled again. "Well, we'll see later on."

There were three people in the group, I suddenly noticed as we got closer, and the third one was Lenore Palmer. She looked very chic, and very much at home, talking animatedly to Gino Amaldi, while Carola Russo stared vacantly at the pool with a look of total boredom on her face.

"Well, here we are!" Neilsen announced in his beautiful deep bass. "You know everybody, of course, Rick. Let me get you a drink?"

"Fine!" I told him, and he moved away from the group briskly, humming to himself as he went.

"Hi, Rick!" Lenore said gaily.

She wore a cheongsam made from a rich silk brocade that shimmered and danced under the strong lights. The high collar and tight fit showed off her figure to full advantage, emphasizing her height and long-stemmed legs, full breasts and narrow waist. Her diamond pendant earrings flashed every time she moved her head, and somehow the short blond hair helped give an almost imperious look to the beautiful oval shape of her face.

By comparison, Carola Russo, wearing a simple black shift that stopped a couple of inches above her knees, should have been completely eclipsed. But it was the redheaded waif, with her full, sensual lips set in a petulant pout and the unexpected thrust of disproportionately large breasts against the straight line of her shift, who caught and held your attention.

Amaldi looked toward me during a brief respite from Lenore's continuous chatter and nodded, then said something in Italian to Carola.

She shrugged listlessly, then turned her head a fraction and looked at me. "Poppa Gino wants to know why the crazy man is back so soon."

"Didn't Neilsen explain why?" I asked her.

"He did, but Poppa Gino didn't listen. That last salvo of yours this morning made him turn his back on the English language forever!"

Neilsen returned and pushed a glass into my hand. "Only another five minutes to go now." His mild blue eyes looked straight into Lenore's face for a moment, and a sudden gleam of panic showed in the convulsive jerk of her head as she looked away.

"You look positively radiant tonight, Lenore!" Neilsen said easily. "The gay life of a bachelor girl obviously suits you! Did you have a chance yet to look around inside the house? I'm having your old room repainted. It will be a much brighter, younger-looking room when it's finished. The way it was before was so depressing, I always thought it had the look of a middle-aged woman, didn't you?"

Lenore bit down onto her lower lip savagely, then shook her head, obviously not trusting herself to speak.

"I like middle-age woman," Amaldi said suddenly. He thrust his massive hands out in front of him, then slowly clenched the fingers. "Nice plump hips," he said dreamily. "Big soft bosom to lie your head! No virgin to scream when you make the little pinch, hey? Middle-age woman she pinch right back at you!" He stood there with a blissful smile on his face, and after a while, the others realized he'd finished monopolizing the conversation.

"Well, it's a provocative thought," Neilsen said in a good-humored voice. "How about that, Lenore? Do you pinch back?"

She made a gallant effort to smile, but she couldn't control her trembling lips any more.

"Ah, well!" Neilsen's voice was sweetly tolerant. "I suppose girls—of all ages!—want to keep some secrets to themselves. How about you, Carola?"

She was staring moodily at the pool, her head turned away from him when he spoke. For maybe five long seconds I thought she wasn't about to answer him, then the four-letter word exploded from her lips. Her eyes still moodily studied the pool; leaving the rest of the group to pick up the splintered remains of the conversation if they wanted.

Neilsen made a big production about checking his watch, then walked quickly away from the group. Lenore took the opportunity to regain her self-control, while Amaldi still smiled blissfully, his fingers clenching and unclenching in an atavistic rhythm. Heaven help the little old ladies if he ever gets loose in Pasadena, I thought wildly, then saw Tino suddenly materialize on the terrace. A couple of seconds later Brunhoff and Martell appeared, and Neilsen hurried to greet them.

"It was real nice of you boys to come!" Neilsen opened his lungs a little, and his deep bass bounced off the back wall of the house and ricochetted around, until it seemed to be coming from all angles at the same time.

"What are these people doing here, Oscar?" Lou Martell asked thinly. "I thought this was going to be a strictly private discussion?"

"So it is, Lou," Neilsen said soothingly. "Everything's ready for us inside the house. These people are my guests, Lou. Allow me to introduce—"

"Forget it!" Lou snapped. "The broads don't matter, the little ape isn't important—what's Holman doing here?"

"A guest, Lou, that's all!" Neilsen patted his shoulder. "Now, why don't the three of us go inside and get down to business?"

They walked slowly back into the house, and a few seconds afterwards, Tino followed them. A heavy silence descended around the terrace, and was finally broken by the sudden rasp of a match.

Carola drew deeply on the cigarette, then sucked down the smoke greedily. "Poppa Gino," she said in a small voice. "For no good reason, I am suddenly scared to death!"

Amaldi opened his eyes with obvious reluctance. "You say something, *cara?*"

Carola swung around toward me, with a sudden gesture of impatience. "Then you tell me why, Rick Holman? You are the great expert on why everybody feels everything!"

I looked hard into her jade-green eyes for a few moments, and said softly, "The hunter is back in the jungle, Carola baby!"

"You're a big help!" she snarled, and turned her back on me again.

The night breeze freshened, and gently ruffled her hair. She shivered suddenly and moved a step closer toward me, then another, so that our shoulders touched.

"I can feel it, moving around out there somewhere," she whispered, nodding toward the solid barrier of darkness that started about twenty feet out from the terrace.

"It's all right," I told her. "Your nerve ends have taken a beating over the last few days, that's all."

Her teeth chattered suddenly. "I know it's out there, Rick, I can feel it!" She closed her eyes tight shut. "You know what it is prowling around out there, don't you? It's Death!"

"It could be my hunter," I said.

"They're the same thing!" She opened her eyes wide and blinked at me slowly. "You knew that all along, didn't you? That's why you said I had to escape the jungle, before the hunter caught up with me!" Her lower lip trembled violently. "But I can't ever leave the jungle, Rick! I don't know how!"

"You know how!" I snarled softly. "Stop being a nothing!"

"You think I can?"

"Sure!" I said confidently. "You—"

There was a furtive, rustling sound from beyond the far side of the pool, just beyond the range of the floodlights. She turned her head quickly toward the spot, her eyes straining to pierce the darkness for a long moment.

"It's too late, Rick!" Her shoulders slumped. "It's still out there, waiting. What was that lovely phrase you used before?" Her nervous laugh sounded more like a cry. "I remember! 'Seeking his predestined prey'!"

"That's me, isn't it?" she whispered, some thirty seconds later.

chapter ten

"I don't *know* why he wants me here tonight!" Lenore said tensely. "But it was the royal command."

"Maybe it's only his usual technique," I said. "Show you your old room that's being repainted, symbolically wiping you out of his life. An opportunity to make all those cheap cracks about middle-aged women—which, incidentally, is so goddamned absurd as a tag for the way you look right now, that nobody even thought he was talking about you!"

"Well—" she smiled wanly "—thanks for that, anyway. How long have they been in there now?"

I looked at my watch. "Nearly two hours."

"Oh God!" She sighed heavily. "You think they'll go on all night?"

"It's a good question!"

She shrugged impatiently. "I'm going to make myself another drink! How about you?"

"Not right now, Lenore."

I moved across to the edge of the terrace where the

110

two high-backed chairs stood side by side. Carola sat bolt upright, her arms wrapped tight around her breasts, staring straight out into the darkness. Beside her, Gino Amaldi snored gently, his thick, fleshy lips quivering every time he exhaled.

"Can I get you a drink?" I asked softly.

"No," she said, shaking her head firmly. "Go away! You make too much noise!"

I moved back toward the temporary bar where Lenore was busy making herself another drink, then stopped when I heard someone walking briskly through the house toward the back terrace.

Oscar Neilsen stepped out from the house maybe five seconds later, and came up to me. His facial expression was exactly the same as it ever was, and didn't tell me a thing.

"It's all over?" I asked him.

"Over," he repeated crisply. "The two men who arrived here as my ex-partners, have just departed the same way!"

"Too bad," I said.

He snapped his fingers contemptuously. "I should have known it would be impossible to reach any kind of agreement with those two avaricious cretins!" He looked at me for a little while, then that beatific smile lit up his whole face.

"Your advice has just been devalued again, Rick!" he said briskly. "I want my nickel back."

It stays in my mind like a motion picture still; that one tiny frame out of the myriad frames that go together to make a movie, locked in the projector gate, so the most minute detail can be examined on the screen.

Oscar Neilsen's face stared into mine, hopeful that the gibe about money might at last provoke some kind of emotional reaction out of me. I could hear the ice-cubes tinkling in Lenore Palmer's freshly made drink; the breeze had freshened a little, and was ruffling the short hairs at the back of my head. Then the explosive sound of the shot split the night; Lenore's glass smashed on the concrete floor, and the whimpering terror in Carola's high-pitched scream tore at my nerve ends as she came face to face with the implacable hunter.

I spun around, dragging the thirty-eight from the belt holster, then reached the edge of the terrace as the second shot exploded, and the gun flash winked at me from somewhere inside the wall of darkness beyond the pool.

"Tino!" Neilsen's powerful voice echoed and thundered, as he rushed into the house. "Tino, they've killed her! You must stop them getting away! Tino!"

I ran from the terrace, around the end of the pool, toward the point in the darkness where the gun flash had momentarily appeared. A third shot sounded and the slug chipped concrete in front of my feet. That flash came from a different point; I realized its source was moving away from me to the left. Under the floodlights I made a beautiful running target; and that thought pounded my legs faster over the concrete until I was through the wall of blackness beyond the range of the lights.

After I'd gotten my breath back, and my eyes were starting to get used to the darkness, I started moving again as quick as I could. A short time later there was a sudden whole fusillade of shots at a distance, someplace in front of the house, I figured.

By the time I'd almost circled around to the front of the house, I guessed any chance of catching up with the killer had long gone. So I moved back into the perimeter of light and stayed there, until I rounded the right-angled corner into the light that flooded from the front porch.

A black sedan lurched at a crazy angle on the edge of the driveway, with broken glass littered all around. Two figures stood close together, looking silently at the wreck; when I got closer they heard my feet crunch on the gravel, and their heads turned toward me.

"That you, Rick?" Neilsen obviously recognized my face at the same moment, and relaxed. "Well, the murdering bastards didn't get away with it," he said bleakly. "If that means anything!"

I went right up to the sedan and peered inside. Sam Brunhoff was slumped forward over the steering wheel, with the back of his head partially blown off. Beyond him, Lou Martell slouched facing me—and the house—across Sam. He was leaning against the car door with an elbow awkwardly propped up in the window behind him and a gun still dangling loosely in his fingers. His face still screamed his silent fury, in spite of the shattered cheekbone and the third eye steadily oozing blood from high in his forehead.

"What happened?" I stepped back from the sedan and looked questioningly at Neilsen.

"I knew Tino was still inside the house," he said, "so I ran inside, yelling for him—"

"I heard you!" I said impatiently. "After that?"

"Tino came out onto the porch, just as Lou Martell came racing back around the house and dived into the car," he said. "Brunhoff had the motor racing, of course, and the moment Lou dived back in, Sam slammed his foot down. Then Tino did the only thing he could to stop them!"

"What did you use?" I muttered. "A tommy gun?"

"Automatic carbine," Tino said softly. "I put it onto *automatic* and sprayed the car—there was nothing else I could do, was there?"

"We'd better get back to the others," Neilsen said savagely. "You never know! There may be a chance there is something we can do for Carola—"

We went back through the house, out onto the terrace again, and the oppressive silence enveloped us like a fog. The lone figure of Lenore Palmer stood in the exact same position she'd been when the first shot was fired. There was no sign of anyone else on the terrace; only the two high-backed chairs placed side by side had a sinister air of expectancy. I walked toward them quickly, then started to run when I heard a faint whimpering sound. Neilsen and Tino were close in back of me, and the three of us got there at about the same time, and came to a sudden halt as we looked down.

Carola Russo sat on the grass in front of the chairs, cradling Amaldi's head fiercely to her bosom, while she whispered to him in snatches of Italian and English, and sometimes just crooned a tuneless melody, between her tears. Poppa Gino was long past caring what she did. The bloodstained front of his coat said both shots had hit him in the chest and he was already dead before the second shot was even fired.

Neilsen knelt down beside Carola, and gently lifted Amaldi's head out of her protective arms. Then he helped her onto her feet. "Come!" he said, with infinite gentleness. "We will look after Gino now." He led her toward the house.

She stopped abruptly after she'd taken a few steps and looked back at me, her jade-green eyes dark and huge in her pinched white face.

"The hunter!" she said thinly. "It wasn't me who was his predestined prey! It wasn't me at all, did you know that?" I shook my head silently, and she continued, "He was hunting Gino all the time—out there in the darkness!—and Gino didn't even know! Little Poppa Gino was fast asleep, snoring, and I kept pinching him to try and wake him up!" She dissolved into tears again, and Neilsen put his arm around her shoulders, then gently pulled her toward the house.

"The hunter who's sitting out front of the house in that sedan was after her, all right!" Tino said in a soft voice. "I wonder if that dame will ever know just how lucky she was! Two chairs side by side—him in one!—her in the other! Over there in the darkness"—he pointed toward the black wall beyond the edge of the pool—"there's Lou with a gun in his hand. Maybe it's a trick of the light, see? They had their backs to it, so their faces would've been in shadow, right, Mr. Holman? Maybe it's because the little fat guy's asleep, and slumped down in his chair he looks smaller than the dame? Whatever it was, Lou puts two slugs through the wrong one's chest!"

"Lucky for Carola," I said slowly, "unlucky for Gino."

Neilsen guided Carola slowly past the rigid figure of Lenore Palmer and into the house. He called over his shoulder to Tino in a soft snarl, "Get some blankets, brandy! She is in shock, you fool!"

"Right away, Mr. Neilsen!" Tino scurried into the house quickly. "Where will I bring them?"

"Her room!" Neilsen said, and there was an undertone of dreadful triumph in his soft-pitched voice.

I reached out and touched Lenore's bare arms; they felt icy-cold. "Are you all right?" I said.

"Did she see his face?" she whispered. "The look on it as he took her into the house?" She shuddered violently. "*Her* room! The one that used to be mine—the one he's had repainted so it was ready and waiting for her!"

Her luminous eyes stared at me in sudden horror. "Oh, my God!" She swayed to one side limply, and I grabbed her just before she fell. "Rick!" Her fingers clutched my lapels and pulled at them fiercely. "Don't you *see*? That's why he wanted me here tonight—to watch the ceremonial installation of his new mistress! He *knew* all this was going to happen!"

"I know," I said quietly. "But only when it was too late to stop it, I knew. I'm going inside the house now, and I'll try to keep them occupied. You think you could get to a phone and call the police?"

"I don't know," she said faintly. "I'll try!"

"Don't rush it," I said. "Wait a few minutes to give me a chance. Have a drink first!"

Lenore nodded, then pushed herself away from me, and held onto the edge of the bar. "I'll be okay, Rick!" she said fiercely. "You go inside."

Once inside the house, I eased the thirty-eight from its holster and held it in my right hand, against my thigh. With a guy like Tino, who most likely had that automatic carbine—and I'd already seen what he could do with it!—still within easy reach of his hand, I didn't figure to be a hero. Ideally, I hoped he'd be looking in the opposite direction when I found him, so I could bounce a gun butt off his skull with relative safety.

I crossed the enormous sunroom with no trouble at all, because its French doors opened straight off the terrace and I could see it was empty before I ventured inside. But the closed door in front me now was a slightly more hazardous proposition. It opened out into the front hall, I knew, but I didn't know if anyone was waiting for me on the other side. Don't get chicken now, I told myself, just open the goddamn thing!

Neilsen and Tino had gone to a fantastic amount of organization to achieve their bloody results, I suddenly remembered. It wouldn't make sense, if they both got careless just at the end. How could they be absolutely sure I'd fallen for it, short of asking me a straightforward question? Well, one easy way was for both of them to disappear inside the house, looking real busy. That would leave me outside on the terrace with somebody to confide in, like Lenore Palmer. Then, if one of them sneaked back and listened for a while, he'd know. I made a convulsive leap to the far side of the closed door and flattened myself against the wall. I reached out awkwardly with my left hand and turned the knob gently, then flung the door open.

Inside the house that carbine sounded like a cannon! It fired three shots in straight succession through the open doorway, and I heard the slug smash into the wood trim and heavy thermoglass of the opposite wall. I counted five in the silence that followed the third shot, then went through the open doorway into the front hall in another convulsive leap. There was a fragmentary, confused impression of the surprise on Tino's face, as he looked up at me over the stock of the carbine from where he lay in another open doorway, diagonally across the hall. My finger triggered the thirty-eight in a kind of conditioned reflex to the sight of his face.

The first slug slammed straight into the carbine's stock, so it splintered right into his face. He screamed once, then the second slug from the thirty-eight punched a hole through the bridge of his nose and he just lay there, his dark eyes wide open and still surprised.

I got smart and went back to the terrace, where Lenore must have heard the shots. I told her what happened, and got detailed instructions on how to find the room that had been hers up until recently. It was way out at the very end of one wing of the house, and I was glad I'd asked for directions by the time I got there.

The door was half-closed so I couldn't see into the room, and there was no sound from inside. I repeated the procedure that had worked nicely for me with the first door. Nothing happened after I flung it open, so I made that convulsive leap into the room with a little more confidence this time.

"You should have knocked, Rick," Neilsen said easily. "I would have told you to just walk in, then!"

His blue eyes watched me with mild interest from the top of the bed where he was sitting comfortably. Carola was stretched out on the same bed, her body rigid with fear—and I would have been scared too if the barrel of Neilsen's gun had been pressed against the side of *my* head.

"Let's do it in the approved style, shall we, Rick?" Neilsen said. "Drop your gun on the floor, then kick it toward me."

I did like he said, and the thirty-eight skidded across the floor and stopped maybe six inches from his right foot.

"Tino must have gotten careless," he rasped.

"Maybe it was me who got extra-cautious?" I said.

"He was a wonderful shot!"

"You know what range it was when he put a bullet into Gallant's shoulder?" I asked interestedly.

"Quiet a distance, anyway!" Neilsen said.

"What happened with Brunhoff and Martell tonight?

You rushed into the house yelling for Tino, to cover him while he got back from somewhere the other side of the pool, after he'd killed Amaldi, right? But where were your two ex-partners right then?"

"Trying to start their car," he said simply. "Tino had made very sure it would never start, of course. I simply walked straight through from the back terrace to the front porch, yelling for Tino to stop them all the way, picked up the carbine waiting beside the open front door, and sprayed the car with bullets."

"It was essential you said it was Tino who'd used the carbine, because it gave him a cast-iron alibi for Amaldi's murder in case he ever needed it," I said. "The gun he used to kill Poppa Gino was the one dangling so dramatically from Lou Martell's lifeless fingers?"

"Naturally!" Neilsen almost chuckled. "Your hindsight is most impressive, Rick!"

"In the beginning," I said. "Lenore saw you were crazy for Carola right from the start, and when Amaldi went back to Rome you started crowding her. She went with Gallant up to the mountains only to escape from you! Lenore tipped off Gino in Rome, and Gallant's wife here, in a fit of pique. When Gino got back from Rome and told you about the cable, you knew it must be Lenore who'd sent it, and she must have tipped off Monica, too.

"You told Lenore to get me; sent Tino up there with his gun to wound Gallant, where it would hurt but wouldn't be serious, and frighten Carola half to death. My guess is, it was only revenge on both of them you wanted then, but the way it worked out, it gave you a wonderful idea. You needed me to substantiate your story all the way through. If you could convince me someone was really gunning for Carola, it shouldn't be too hard to murder Amaldi at some later stage and make everyone believe the gun was aimed at the girl."

"Brilliant hindsight, as I said before, Rick." He yawned gently.

"You gave me a nice gentle steer toward your ex-partners as the most likely villains in the piece," I went on bleakly. "Knowing in advance that I could never find anything conclusive, so if I didn't advise you finally to make a deal with your ex-partners, I'd certainly agree it was a logical solution if you suggested it. I just wish I didn't make myself look so goddamn stupid in the telling!" I growled.

"It's all history now, Rick, anyway." He looked at me thoughtfully. "The last important question is—what happens now?"

"The decision is your privilege while you're holding that gun against Carola's head," I said carefully. "But I'd like to point up a couple of things first, if I may?"

"You know I enjoy hearing you think out loud, Rick?" he said blandly. "It always gives me such confidence in my own reasoning powers."

"If you kill the girl, I'll jump you before you've got the chance of a second shot," I said politely. "To kill me first, you've got to take the gun away from the girl's head; I know Carola would prefer to die than be left to your loving care, so once you remove the gun from her head she will either make a grab for it, or push your arm—you know?"

"You make it sound very convincing, Rick!" There was a contemptuous sneer in his voice. "Either way, I'm left deep in a quandary, or perched high on the horns of a dilemma? Well, supposing we just stay as we are now for a while?"

"That's fine by me," I said sincerely. "It must be at least ten minutes after the time Lenore called the police."

His mouth tightened around the corners perceptibly. "I wonder how I managed to put myself into such an unhealthy situation in the first place?"

"That's easy!" I smiled confidently "Because you're a nut!"

"Please, no vulgarities, Rick!"

"You're right," I apologized. "It was not only rude, but incorrect. The right word is *stupid!*"

"Coming from you, that's very funny!" he rasped.

"You were stupid from the very beginning," I said easily. "Stupid to think you could ever own a girl like Carola, when you knew her flesh would creep whenever you walked into the same room! When she went off to a love nest in the mountains with a slob like Gallant in preference to having you chase her around a hotel suite, you should have got the message then, Oscar. But you didn't, because you're stupid, right?"

The blandness wore out of his face as he stared at me, and the mask of cold implacable fury set hard in its place.

"The most stupid thing of all was to bring Lenore Palmer here for the ceremonial casting-off of the old mistress and ritualistic installation of the new. That was a luxury, Oscar, and nobody who plans a triple murder in one night can afford luxuries too!

"Lenore couldn't help but figure it out by herself— if you brought her here to see the new mistress installed, you must have known in advance it was going to happen. But you could never make Carola your mistress while Amaldi was alive—and that meant you also knew in advance that he was going to die. It doesn't fit too well with the theory he was shot by mistake, and the intended victim was Carola, does it?"

"I'm tired of listening to your stupid, whining voice. Holman!" the long-suppressed fury inside him suddenly bubbled over. "You conceited, pathetic moron! I led you by the nose from the very beginning of this!"

"What are you trying to prove, Oscar baby?" I yawned openly. "That you're not a creep? You want to check with Carola first, baby!"

His whole body started to shake in fury, and a glazed filmy look came into his eyes. "That's enough!" His voice trembled. "I won't stand any more, Holman, you understand?"

"Just a question, Oscar?" I said contemptuously. "Now I've successfully provoked an emotional reaction out of you—that means I've got my hooks sunk deep into your little white underbelly right now, doesn't it?

He screamed an obscenity at me, then jerked the gun barrel away from the side of Carola's head and swung it toward me in a wild arc. Carola lashed out viciously, and her arm collided with his; so the gun now pointed at the corner of the room instead of me. I dived toward him and he thought I was grabbing for his gun, so he leaped sideways out of my reach, then flattened himself against the wall.

It wasn't his gun that primarily interested me, it was my own that still lay on the floor beside the bed. I scooped it up in my right hand, as I landed on the floor chest-first, then frantically jerked my wrist upwards.

Neilsen got the first shot because he'd had a little more time, but I guessed with all that emotion pounding through him it was hard to aim straight. The slug from his gun went through the bottom of the bed, missing Carola's left ankle by a couple of inches, and buried itself in the floor.

Holman got the second shot, and the third, because he didn't have any more time; the first one hit Neilsen a little high in the chest, and the second in the head because he was falling forward at the time.

I helped Carola up off the bed and out of the room. Lenore had been skulking around the first bend in the hallway, halfway out of her mind, and she was happy to take over the job of looking after Carola. They got a little ahead of me when I stopped to light a cigarette; and right then I remembered one small thing I still had to do.

Oscar Neilsen's body had half-rolled when it hit the floor, so he lay on his side with his face—that I had once thought of as saintlike—turned toward the door. Death had stamped the distorted snarl on his face permanently, and Oscar just didn't look very attractive at all. I dug a handful of change out of my pants pocket, found a nickel, and tossed it across the room. It landed on his forehead, bounced onto the bridge of his nose, then slid over his top lip and got wedged in one corner of the snarling mouth.

"Now I owe you nothing!" I said.

Janie Trent looked at me with a serious expression on her pixie face. "But why did those dreadful policemen keep you locked up all night, Rick? You were practically a hero!"

"Not to them, baby," I said bleakly. "They got landed with four corpses, a couple of semihysterical dames—and me! Which would you pick on?"

"Why, you, lover!" She smiled fondly. "Anyway, how was it? I mean they didn't beat you with little rubber hoses, or anything?"

"Just with the responsibilities that go along with the privilege of holding a private detective's license," I said miserably. "I think if I'd had the choice, I would've preferred the little rubber hoses."

"But they let you go this morning, so it must be all right?" she persisted.

"It's all right now," I said. "But think how it was *then?*"

"You've had a bad time, lover, and I'll make it up to you!" She sealed the bargain by taking a chunk out of my nearest earlobe with her needle-sharp teeth.

"Don't do that!" I protested.

"You'd rather I did this?" Her smile was all sweetness and light as she sank her nails cruelly into my bare chest.

"I give in!" I yelped. "I surrender!"

"Of course!" She rolled over onto her stomach and leaned her elbows on my chest, cupped her chin in her hands, then looked down at me with casual interest. "Did I tell you about Monica Hayes?"

"Not lately," I moaned.

"She walked out on Don three days back!" Janie said

excitedly. "She's definitely going for a divorce, she told me, and it made me feel so guilty I had to confess to her I'd had a secret affair with her husband for a while. I suddenly felt all noble, and said if she wanted to use me as the corespondent, it was okay by me!"

"And is she?" I mumbled.

"No, she's got a couple of dozen names already. But the thing is she forgave me freely, because she'd known about it all the time, and it hadn't worried her at all. What's a best friend for, if she can't share the odd husband here and there, she said!" Janie beamed down at me, "Wasn't that nice?"

"She's a kook!" I snarled. "You're a kook! If you have to lean something of yours on my chest, can't you do any better than a pair of lousy elbows?"

"Okay," she said happily. She shuffled around for a few moments, "How's that?"

"A vast improvement!" I sighed contentedly.

"I'm not sure I like that 'vast' bit?—Monica must have walked out the morning of the same day you tagged Don with that sexy nurse?" Janie prattled on. "How about that?"

"If the only way to shut up for a while is to make violent love to you, baby," I said in a resigned voice, "then I'm prepared to—Hey!"

"Don't do that!" she said sharply. "When you make a sudden leap like that, I don't know what's happening to me all over the place!"

"If Monica walked out that morning," I said slowly, "maybe Don and that sexy nurse have been alone together in the house ever since?"

"How about that?" Her hazel eyes twitched with feminine curiosity, which was almost as strong as mine.

"The phone's your side of the bed," I told her.

"But it's on top of the bureau, Rick!" She gave me her sad, sad look. "I'll catch cold walking over there without any clothes on!"

"And I'll catch a fever watching you do it," I growled.

"Out you go!" I gave her an encouraging slap across her nicely upholstered rump.

She squealed across to the bureau, grabbed the phone, and squealed hopefully all the way back again.

"You know the number—dial it," I told her.

"You do the talking?"

"Deal!"

Janie dialed the number, then handed me the phone. It rang for quite a while and I was about to hang up, when I heard a click.

"Yes?" a feminine voice sighed dreamily in my ear.

"I just wanted to confirm a report that Mr. Gallant's been tied up in a featured role the last few days?" I said pleasantly. "I understand it's one of those nurse-patient epics?"

"I'm not sure if I should confirm or deny the report," she said languorously. "But I can tell you this, there's a serious lag in the schedule that has to be caught up, so the whole unit will be working night and day over the next week or so!"

"Thank you," I told her. "How's Mr. Gallant's shoulder?"

"Coming along nicely!"

"And how's Mr. Gallant?"

"Well," she said with something even stronger than maternal affection. "He's lost a little weight and that's made him a little melancholy, but he'll see the schedule through, I can personally guarantee it."

"Thanks again," I told her. "Goodbye."

"You don't know—" she coughed delicately "—by any chance, what ever happened to his wife?"

"She's divorcing him," I said.

"Oh, thanks," she said warmly. "Only yesterday Mr. Gallant wondered where she went."

I put down the phone, and a bundle of assorted feminine charms sprawled all over me.

"Okay, Holman!" Janie said grimly. "Quit fooling around. We've got a schedule to lick!"

"I'm your man," I told her, "but only under one condition. If I start getting melancholy, you call that nurse for me!"

Janie gave a wild shriek and rolled right off the bed. It was a hell of a good start to the schedule!

SIGNET Thrillers You Will Enjoy

A VERY PRIVATE ISLAND   **by Z. Z. Smith**

This taut story of a man trapped on an island with a killer is top-drawer suspense right up to its dramatic finish.
(#D2186—50¢)

DON'T JUST STAND THERE, DO SOMEONE
by Don Von Elsner

A scheming beauty queen takes suave lawyer, David Danning, for a ride that leads straight to blackmail and murder. (#S2134—35¢)

DEATH ON LOCATION   **by William R. Cox**

Murder stalks a carefree movie set on location in Las Vegas. (#S2158—35¢)

CALAMITY FAIR   **by Wade Miller**

A rapid-fire, corpse-strewn thriller about a ruthless blackmail ring that frames lovely ladies—and almost ends the career of Max Thursday, one of America's most popular fictional detectives. (#S1991—35¢)

DON'T BETRAY ME   **by John Berry**

Set in France, 1962, the harrowing story of an assassin who turns a home into a household of terror.
(#S2241—35¢)

THE CRUMPLED CUP   **by Henry Kane**

A teen-age "Lolita" keeps a rendezvous with death on a deserted beach. (#G2301—40¢)

THE PRAYING MANTISES   **by Hubert Monteilhet**

A gripping novel of suspense, acclaimed in both France and America as the best mystery novel of the year, in 1962. (#D2308—50¢)

KILLER'S CHOICE (Devil On Two Sticks)   **by Wade Miller**

A taut, high-powered story of big-time organized crime as a powerful syndicate boss goes after the high-placed informer who was squealing right to the Attorney General. (#S1964—35¢)

THE KILROY GAMBIT   by Irwin R. Blacker

A top-secret Washington agency has to battle meddling congressmen as well as enemy agents to accomplish its mission of Cold War espionage.   (#S2063—35¢)

FATAL STEP   by Wade Miller

A hard-boiled private eye stalks a cold-blooded gunman through the tawdry glitter and eerie shadows of an amusement park ". . . brisk . . . explosive . . . high bracket toughum."—*Saturday Review*.   (#S1911—35¢)

THE DEEP   by Mickey Spillane

Spillane, at his rough and tough best, provides a shock of an ending for this thriller about a man bent on settling a broken pact.   (#D2044—50¢)

JUST NOT MAKING MAYHEM LIKE THEY USED TO
by Don Von Elsner

Colonel Danning tries to crack a cruel extortion racket in this thriller featuring the brilliant sleuth who made his first appearance in *Those Who Prey Together, Slay Together*.   (#S2040—35¢)

UNEASY STREET   by Wade Miller

A baffling, tough, action-packed chiller about private eye Max Thursday who tangled with a vicious smuggling syndicate and a dangerous blonde when he delivered a box packed with a hundred grand.   (#G2317—40¢)

DEATH OF A DASTARD   by Henry Kane

A Casanova who blackmails his lady-loves ends up a corpse, and private-eye Peter Chambers is called on to save a seductive millionairess from the death sentence.   (#G2329—40¢)

THE BEST READING AT REASONABLE PRICES

signet paperbacks

SIGNET BOOKS *Leading bestsellers, ranging from fine novel plays, and short stories to the best entertain ment in the fields of mysteries, westerns, popula biography and autobiography, as well as timel non-fiction and humor. Among Signet's outstand ing authors are winners of the Nobel and Pulitze Prizes, the National Book Award, the Anisfield Wolf award, and many other honors.*

SIGNET SCIENCE LIBRARY *Basic introductions to the variou fields of science — astronomy physics, biology, anthropology, mathematics, an others—for the general reader who wants to kee up with today's scientific miracles. Among th authors are Irving Adler, Isaac Asimov, an Ashley Montagu.*

SIGNET REFERENCE AND SIGNET KEY BOOKS *A dazzlin array of dic tionaries, thesauri, self-taught languages, and othe practical handbooks for the home library, includ ing nature guides, guides to colleges, bridge, job hunting, marital success, and other personal an family interests, hobbies, and problems.*

SIGNET CLASSICS *The most praised new imprint in paper bound publishing, presenting masterwork by writers of the calibre of Mark Twain, Sincla Lewis, Dickens, Hardy, Hawthorne, Thorea Conrad, Tolstoy, Chekhov, Voltaire, George O well, and many, many others, beautifully printe and bound, with handsome covers. Each volum includes commentary by a noted scholar or criti and a selected bibliography.*